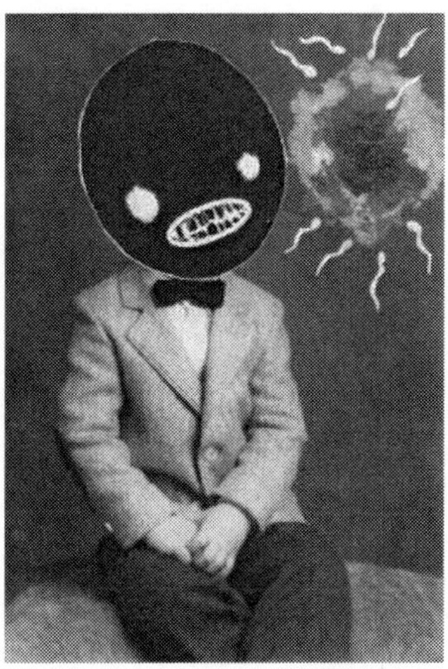

The Self-Esteem Holocaust Comes Home

Sam Pink

Lazy Fascist Press
Portland, OR

LAZY FASCIST PRESS
830 SW 18TH AVENUE
PORTLAND, OR 97205

WWW.LAZYFASCIST.COM

ISBN: 1-936383-35-7

Printed in the USA.

for gianni

(and for the person reading it)

CONTENTS

THE BASTARDS [THEY TRAVEL IN QUIET — WITH THE HOLY FATHER LANDING CREW]

Night. Three policemen, driving. They travel in quiet. The driver blows out smoke from his cigarette, hand against his face, other hand lightly attending the steering wheel. Lights from the dash green his face. And the other two policemen—one in the passenger side, one in the backseat—they are quiet. They stop at an abandoned school building cuffed with snow.

THE DRIVER: Here it is [*throws cigarette out the window*] This is where The World's Greatest Dad sleeps.

THE PASSENGER: [*making circles in fogged window with fingertips*] I have so many questions. I'm a confused person [*breathes fog to cover circles*] I'm just glad we're here. It's safe here. Do you guys agree?

Nobody answers. They leave the car and cross the playground. One of the policemen spins the tic-tac-toe panels as he walks by. Another policeman falls on some ice, then gets up, very slow and mechanic. The school is lit by what little light comes from the streetlight and each of the empty brick windowells is a black rectangle. The policemen pause in front of the school, staring.

THE DRIVER: [*finger to his lips*] Shh. The building is sleeping. We should be quiet. If it wakes up, it will eat us whole. All of us.

THE PASSENGER: Yeah, everyone be quiet.

All three are still staring at the school.

THE MAN FROM THE BACKSEAT: My face is the least quiet part of my body. Unless wait, does your voice come from your face or from your stomach? Whatever. I will try to keep both quiet [*puts a hand on each's shoulder*] I don't want you guys to dislike me. I want to remain friends. I have so many questions for The Greatest Dad in the World. I'm just so excited. This is Heaven. Ok, I'll be quiet now, sorry. Ok.

THE DRIVER: I don't believe in Heaven. I only believe in hands that are everywhere. You can get in the hands if you want a ride up. You can get in the hands if you just want to move. The hands are everywhere. But they don't ever know where they're going, ever. And they don't make you get in either.

They disappear into a black doorway on the side of the school and enter a room floored by garbage, some streetlight imported through the empty window. There is a man sleeping on the ground, hair and beard dreadlocked, shoes flapped open. He sleeps on his side, dirty coat for a blanket on his legs. The decal on the front of his sweatshirt reads 'Greatest Dad in the World.' And the ground is silted filth displaced by his body.

THE MAN FROM THE BACKSEAT: [*to the driver*] You were right. There are hands everywhere [*excited*] We are the hands. We have to be the hands. Should we carry him up?

THE DRIVER: [*kneels*] No. No, he is too good for our hands. We have been with the dirt in the woods. We have been with the dirt. Right now we are the filth under him. He is too good for our hands. We have to learn from him first. Then we will be clean enough to carry him to Heaven or up or wherever. Or just keep lifting him because we don't know where to go.

THE MAN FROM THE BACKSEAT: [*quietly*] We don't know where we're going.

THE PASSENGER: We don't know what we're doing.

The driver gently kicks the chest of The Greatest Dad in the World, toes against the decal. Then flashlights him.

THE DRIVER: Hey, wake up [*pause*] We have questions for you, wise one.

Eyes open, The Greatest Dad in the World tenses and sprawls out. He grabs a garbagebag nearby. Then he eyes the policemen with an animal distrust. Loses sight of them in the flashlight.

THE DRIVER: [*waves flashlight back and forth*] Relax, motherfucker, I don't want your cans. I want to ask you some questions—you know, since my father was shitty by comparison [*clears throat*] Alright. Um let's see. Are the hands really everywhere and are we clean enough to sleep in them? [*sniffs*] Will the hands help us? Are we the hands? And would you like us to carry you up or no? [*nervous*] Wait. Tell me about the hands. I guess just, wait, tell me about the hands please. Do that first please.

THE PASSENGER: [*nudging forward*] Greatest Dad in the World, what is my true calling in life? Am I able to accomplish it? Who is this person I call me? [*laughs*]

THE MAN FROM THE BACKSEAT: [*standing on tip toes to ask over their shoulders*] Am I incapable of loving another human being or is everyone incapable of doing that and I'm just worried about nothing? [*looks at other policemen*] Sorry is it my turn yet?

THE DRIVER: [*chopping the air once for emphasis*] Wait. We're being selfish. It's too cold out to be this selfish. We can drive him around and he can answer our questions and we can buy him food. And make him warm. We need to warm him up in the car before he can answer our questions. I think we need to stop being so selfish [*chops air again*] That's what I think [*flashlight dies*] Shit.

The Greatest Dad in the World collects his things and claps out of the room on his broken shoes. He glances over his shoulder at them all before the outside takes him. The policemen move towards the same lit doorframe, and follow him outside.

THE DRIVER: [*pushing The Greatest Dad in The World into the snow*] Get in the car.

They pick him up and push him into the passenger seat. They get in too, the passenger taking a seat in back. Everyone is quiet. They idle in the parking lot with the heater on all the way.

THE DRIVER: Greatest Dad in the World, are you feeling warmer and better now? Really—have we been helpful?

The Greatest Dad in the World says nothing.

THE MAN FROM THE BACKSEAT: [*leaning forward from backseat*] Good, then—am I a good boy? [*warning*] Be honest. I need to know. Just tell me [*breathes out, straightens himself*] Have I been a good boy or not?

THE DRIVER: [*puts hand on passenger-side headrest*] I already called the first question. Greatest Dad in the World, what did you want to be when you grew up, before you became a person without a home? I want to know that.

The Greatest Dad in the World says nothing. He faces his lap. The policemen all stare at him.

THE GREATEST DAD IN THE WORLD: [*long pause, soft coughing*] I wanted to fly airplanes.

THE MAN FROM THE BACKSEAT: Wait, what did he say. I can't hear because of the heater. Get him to say it again.

THE PASSENGER: He said he wanted to do airplane shit.

THE MAN FROM THE BACKSEAT: What does airplane shit mean.

THE GREATEST DAD IN THE WORLD: Airplanes. Flying airplanes.

THE DRIVER: [*turning off headlights*] Oh oh, ok. That's great, Greatest Dad in the World. I am proud [*pokes*] of [*pokes*] you [*pokes, takes a deep breath, shrugs*] You didn't learn how to do that [*releases shrug*] but that's ok I think [*cranes neck towards back windshield*] Or wait, did you just park your plane around the corner and I can't see it? [*taps Greatest Dad with back of hand*] Hey, when am I going to be on a plane and hear the Greatest Dad in the World on the p.a.? [*puts his hand up to his mouth, mimics sound of scratchy speaker*] "This is, Captain Greatest Dad in the World, on the p-fucking-a. Just wanted to let you know, if you look to the left, you'll see my bag of cans. And also, I am better than every dad on this flight. Turn to your dad and tell him that [*makes static clicking sound*] Over."

THE MAN FROM THE BACKSEAT: [*looking at the driver*] So is he going to answer our questions? Can I go, can I ask? [*leans over*] Hey are you going to answer our questions?

THE GREATEST DAD IN THE WORLD: I don't know what you're talking about.

THE PASSENGER: [*reaches forward, lowers the window by The Greatest Dad in the World*] Hey, can you wipe off that frost? I can't see out that window. I need to see the outside or I'll feel trapped. It's weird, but just, can you do it?

The Greatest Dad in the World puts his hand out the window and rubs the frost with his fingers. He holds the bag of cans and plastic bottles tightly and scratches the frost off. The driver rolls the window up, crushing The Greatest Dad in the World's fingers. Blood leaks down the window on both sides.

THE DRIVER: Window got your fingers? [*turns to policemen in backseat, gesturing vaguely*] See it's like 'cat got your tongue?' but instead of a tongue it's your fingers and instead of a cat it's a window. You guys get it?

THE PASSENGER: Guys, are we going to be fair about asking questions? Are we each going to take turns? I will wait if you promise that we'll get to me eventually. Let's just fucking be fair for once huh. All right? Good for everyone?

THE DRIVER: [*leaning towards face of The Greatest Dad in the World*] Airplanes, airplanes. You really have to be a big strong guy to handle an airplane. Are you a strong guy? We know you're a great guy [*smiles*] But are you a strong guy?

The Greatest Dad in the World holds his trapped arm and winces.

THE DRIVER: Oh, that's good [*pause, taps steering wheel with fingers*] That is, good stuff [*leaning, he tests a bicep muscle with his fingers*] Oh man, whew. Who hid a rock in your coat? I hate to be the one to tell you, but someone hid a rock in your coat here. Maybe we should all look to arrest whoever hid the rock here. Or arrest you for impersonating a man with rock-arms.

THE PASSENGER: [*laughs through nose*] Look out [*leans forward*] Hey I want my seat back.

THE GREATEST DAD IN THE WORLD: [*erratic breaths*] I can't feel the snow on my fingers now. It's there but I can't feel it [*wincing*] Please let me go.

THE DRIVER: When I look at your fingers I am reminded that nothing is beautiful [*stops, then almost whispering*] What have I become? Greatest Dad in the World, I want you to stay with us and tell me, what have I become?

Someone walks by the car, then they are gone into the distance. And a freight train passes, loud, just two blocks away.

THE DRIVER: I want you to listen to me. Are you listening? Huh, Captain? Are you listening? We need help. We [*pause*] are bad people. But we want to be good people [*pointing*] You can help us. You have to help us.

THE MAN FROM THE BACKSEAT: Captain Greatest Dad in the world, lead us safely to the ground. Please, we don't want our lives to be over this quickly. Help us be good people. The bad people are reaching out to you. Get in our hands.

The Greatest Dad in the World winces, slouches. He is touching the trapped arm. He moves his fingers slowly and watches them through the window. Can't breathe.

GREATEST DAD IN THE WORLD: [*hoarse*] God.

THE DRIVER: I want you to hear this—God wants you to hear this [*mimics p.a. sound again*] Hear me. Captain Greatest Dad in the World, Captain Greatest Dad in the World [*makes static sound*] this is the landing crew. This is God. Do you read me? God the Landing Crew to the Greatest Dad in the World. Do you read? Over. Need confirmation. I repeat, need confirmation. [*makes static sound*]

The policemen all laugh.

THE PASSENGER: You were always the funny one [*then suddenly not laughing*]

THE DRIVER: [*still smiling*] Take my wife. Take her and bury her next to the Greatest Dad in the World.

THE MAN FROM THE BACKSEAT: [*drumming on thighs, nervous and cold*] I don't get that one.

THE DRIVER: Greatest Dad in the World, why do I immediately feel angered by almost everyone I meet [*turns slightly in seat*] Is it just because I really want to be friends with them and I can't, so I act mean? [*confused*] Why am I like that?

THE PASSENGER: Wait [*looking at driver*] do I make you angry?

THE MAN FROM THE BACKSEAT: [*leaning forward*] Yeah, how about me?

THE DRIVER: [*gesturing*] No I mean everyone else. Come on. We're great friends. Right?

THE PASSENGER and THE MAN FROM THE BACKSEAT: [*together*] Yeah.

They sit quietly. Slats of cold come in through the window that has crushed the fingers.

THE MAN FROM THE BACKSEAT: Greatest Dad in the World, is it better to learn something or already know it?

GREATEST DAD IN THE WORLD: [*grabbing wrist with other hand, pulls*] I don't know.

They watch someone slide past on a bike, a single light on its handlebars guiding the bike into the distance's eventual darkness.

THE DRIVER: [*watching the bike leave*] What are those called again?

THE MAN FROM THE BACKSEAT: Bicycles?

THE PASSENGER: Yeah bicycles. Greatest Dad in the World, will my kids grow up to hate me? [*clears throat*] Am I being a good dad myself? I mean [*raises both hands*] clearly, I can't be the best. But you know.

THE DRIVER: Oh also, I forgot, watch this [*hits his hand against the seat, dust emerges*] I can't figure out how that gets in there. I mean, there is so much. Sorry [*looks around*] is it my turn? Every time I hit the seat more of it comes out. It's inside and always floating out. There must be mating. What does the mating look like? I would catch it in my mouth if I weren't worried about it killing me. I wish I was inside the seat and that there were no hands to knock me out. I don't want to die. I do not want to die without knowing I have done good [*scratches chin*] Sorry, that was more than one question.

THE PASSENGER: [*to no one*] No one ever gave me Valentine's cards in grade school. That is why I am so mean and angry.

THE MAN FROM THE BACKSEAT: [*to the passenger*] I liked the ones with a word game on them.

THE DRIVER: Me too [*to man from the backseat*] Hey are you tired man? You look all tired lately.

THE MAN FROM THE BACKSEAT: Naw [*seems to question self*] I'm good.

THE DRIVER: Alright [*looking at The Greatest Dad in the World, still addressing the man from the backseat*] You should sleep more though. It's good for you. At least eight hours they say. They say at least eight hours, right? [*poking Greatest Dad*] I can't have my little guys sleepy all the time. We are so very excited about being awake.

The Greatest Dad in the World cries softly. He clenches up and looks at his fingers. Then he tugs them through the window in three quick pulls and they slide through, some ripping off. The hand drops heavy into his lap, fingers bent red and blue, with pasty white folds where the skin is crumpled.

THE DRIVER: [*looking forward at the snow-cuffed school*] Please don't leave us [*very soft*] Just don't leave. Not now. We need—

The Greatest Dad in the World kicks his boot into the driver's mouth, sending the driver's head into the window hard. Then he elbows the man from the backseat when the man from the backseat tries to lean forward. The elbow breaks his nose and The Greatest Dad in the World grabs the ice scraper by his feet. He shoves the scraper end of the ice scraper into the passenger's mouth as the passenger comes forward trying to strangle him. The ice scraper rips from the corner of his mouth fully to the ear, and he chokes on the scream, leaning back with his hands over his face. The Greatest Dad in the World fails to open the door with his broken fingers, so he switches hands and pushes his broken fingers into the backseat, into the passenger's ripped cheek, along the gumline. And, rip-faced, the passenger bites down hard, missing, the broken fingers slipping along his gums. The car door opens, and The Greatest Dad in the World runs into the darkness. Out through the playground of the school and into an alley he dots the snow, looking up and down the roads and corners. Running. The flakes come heavy and slow. He is The Greatest Dad in the World and he has a big future. In the car the policemen sit in harsh draft and flake fall.

THE DRIVER: [*through bloody mouth*] Hey uh [*shakes head*] I don't know about you guys, but, I'm not going to run. Just let him go. I'm toot ired.

THE PASSENGER: [*holding his ripped face together*] Did you say "too tired" or "toot ired."

THE DRIVER: [*turning head*] What?

THE MAN FROM THE BACKSEAT: It seems stupid that we all just passed up an opportunity to learn from The Greatest Dad in the World. What will we do now? There is no greater dad than him [*ruffles bag of cans*] He won't even be a father to this bag of cans and bottles. I didn't even know you could be the father of some cans and plastic bottles. We need to put the bags of cans and bottles before ourselves. See? That's our problem [*nodding, earnest*] We're selfish.

THE DRIVER: It has been proven that cans and plastic bottle that grow up in a home with a father are less likely to resort to crime. Him being the greatest dad makes that even more true. We should adopt them.

THE PASSENGER: [*coughs, blood comes out through his hand, down his arm*] We can find him if we follow the footsteps he left on the ground [*gets out of car*] Come on.

He shines the blue light of his phone onto the snow, holds his face together with the other hand.

THE DRIVER: Hey you guys this may seem weird but last night I sat in my room trying to fall asleep and I kept grinding my teeth as hard as I could—really really fucking hard [*looking at blue lit footsteps*] and when I woke up my face and neck hurt. I sucked out the clots from beneath each tooth and that was my breakfast hallelujah [*shaking head, laughs*] Alright, let's go. We can go.

They crouch and follow the phone-lit footsteps of The Greatest Dad in the World. And they travel in quiet.

BE NICE TO EVERYONE [VERSION 1]

A male and a female are taking a shower together in a small cold bathroom. The female runs her hair beneath the showerhead and then squeezes the water out.

FEMALE: Are you done?

MALE: [*looking at his feet*] Yes.

The female shuts the water off and steps out of the shower. She begins to towel off. The male stays in the shower, watching the water drain.

FEMALE: [*toweling hair*] Why are you still standing there?

MALE: Do you ever worry that something is leaving with the water? [*holds elbows*] And that it will never come back?

FEMALE: Not at all.

They both stand there until the water drains. The only sound is the fan taking the steam out of the room. The male gets out and takes the towel from her and dries off, still thinking that something is bothering him and that it may have nothing to do with the water draining.

MALE: Maybe I owe the water an apology.

The male and the female put their underwear on and face the mirror. The only sound is the fan.

MALE: [*reaching past her to grab deodorant*] I love you more than anything.

FEMALE: [*combing hair, making eye contact with him in mirror*] Hey, can you hand me that lipstick on the windowsill behind you?

MALE: [*turning*] Here you go.

FEMALE: Thanks, I think— [*she stops and looks at her hand then holds a shard of glass up to the mirror*] Nice try. Nice. Try. You think this would kill me? [*slowly, evenly*] You will ne-ver kill me. You will never be alone. You will never say goodbye to me. And you. Will never. Be alone.

The male twists his chesthair, nervous.

MALE: That is one of my worries [*looking up*] I hate you. But I am content with staying with you until you die or turn against me, rather than trying to leave you now. Because I am very weak. And I try not to hurt other peoples' feelings. Those two things make my life long. Those two things don't leave with the water.

The female looks at him in the mirror. Puts on her deodorant.

FEMALE: Why do you feel that way? [*switches arms*] Why do you have feelings? I don't have any feelings—at all. Ever. I don't have any feelings. How do you feel right now? Tell me.

The male puts the toilet lid down and sits on it.

MALE: I feel like an elderly man who committed suicide with a handgun and died face down on a quilt his dead wife made for him.

A long pause. They remain facing opposite directions.

FEMALE: You will never be alone.

MALE: [*looking at his feet*] Stop saying that. It can't be true.

They leave the bathroom and enter the female's bedroom. The male turns on the ceilingfan light. The words "YOU'RE DEAD" are projected on the wall.

FEMALE: Hey, what the fuck.

MALE: Yeah, I wrote "YOU'RE DEAD" on the lightbulb. It took me a few lightbulbs to get it legible. I mean, I didn't really have anything else to do this afternoon.

The blinds hit against the window and the female is nervous, looking at the walls and the blinds and anything else with distinct features. She looks at the words "YOU'RE DEAD" on the wall and turns to the window, trying not to cry. The face she makes while trying not to cry should not be seen by anyone. She looks through the window at the forest preserve in the distance.

FEMALE: [*slowly composed*] I used to ride my bike back there [*craning her neck*] Until I got molested by a man with a raincoat on [*laughing*] I heard that fucker got shot last week because the police thought he was reaching into his pants for a gun. That makes me feel good [*tone lightens*] But everybody gets molested though. So it's cool. I don't hate him. He was my dad. I have to love him.

The male looks out the window. He appears to be thinking.

MALE: Huh. Did the man in a raincoat have soft hands? Or what.

FEMALE: [*not facing the male*] Yes he did. He had very soft hands.

MALE: Everybody gets molested [*pause*] Do you have any chapstick? I can still taste one of your kisses.

The female reaches into a drawer.

FEMALE: Yeah here.

MALE: [*undoes lid*] Hey, you didn't poison this at all or anything? Huh?

The female refuses to look. And a man in a raincoat appears a foot from the window. He is not smiling.

MALE: Come on, you have to tell me if I ask. Did you poison this?

FEMALE: [*pause*] Alright. Yes. I did. I crushed up some rat poison and sprinkled it on. It's because you leave all the time. I'm sorry.

The male tosses the chapstick to the ground.

MALE: That's ok. At least you were honest. I just wanted you to be honest.

FEMALE: [*turning to him*] It was just a little poison. You would've been fine, ultimately.

The female's cat runs up behind the male, bites his toe.

MALE: [*holds foot*] Fuck.

THE CAT: [*looking up*] Reer.

MALE: [*looking down*] I didn't know that.

THE CAT: Reer.

MALE: Well that remains to be determined.

THE CAT: Reer.

MALE: Now you're just being an asshole.

THE CAT: Reer.

The cat bites the male's toe again then runs away.

MALE: [*to the female*] I will forgive the cat because the cat's brain has maybe like two folds in it. Its brain can't accomplish much [*turns*] Oh hey [*reaching into backpack on floor, hands the female a wrapped present*] Here you go. I forgot I bought you a present today. When I saw these, I totally thought of you. I had to get them. This is for reminding me I will never be alone.

FEMALE: [*opening present, looking at the male*] I'm so excited.

When she's finished removing the paper, she opens the box and finds two frogs with rubber bands wrapped tightly around their necks. They are motionless. The female sits on the bed and cries. She drops the box. The male puts his shoes on to leave. He appears disgusted. A breeze pulls the blinds against the windowframe again.

FEMALE: [*wiping her face, sniffling*] Hey, I tried that toothpaste you were bragging about. I tried the supposedly great toothpaste you bought.

MALE: [*hand on the doorknob, turning*] Yeah?

FEMALE: Yeah it's not that fucking great. I think you exaggerated. I think you were trying to impress me.

MALE: [*opens door*] So what?

The female stands, her face close to the window. Close to the man in the raincoat opposite.

FEMALE: So you said it was so great. It's not. It's just ok, not great. You're a lame human. And you will be afraid of how much you hate me [*looks to him*] You will never be alone.

MALE: That can't be true [*pause*] That can't be true. I think you will miss me.

FEMALE: That can't be true. You will not be spared.

The male looks at her. A long moment. He looks between the doorknob and her. Then he leaves, down the hallway. By the stairs at the end of the hallway, he encounters an old man. The old man is sawing his own head off and he's about halfway done.

YOU CAN'T CONTROL A KITE

Two men sit in a booth at a fast food restaurant, waiting for their order. QNNQR sits on one side, and KWWKQ on the other side. Their faces are blurred out. Everyone in the restaurant has a blurred out face. And outside through the window, there's a giant inflatable gorilla in the parking lot of a car dealership. QNNQR flicks some fries off the table.

QNNQR: I bet you suck at mini-golf.

KWWKQ: [*watching the fries hit the ground and slide, spinning*] No doubt, man. No doubt. Not patient enough.

QNNQR: [*still flicking fries*] Exactly.

Someone walks by and steps on one of the fries that was flicked to the ground, keeps walking. Both men look at the smashed fry, unflinching. A homeless man takes a seat at the table next to them, and rests his head in his arms. He sleeps.

QNNQR: Hey, how many times a day would you say you masturbate to hardcore pornography?

KWWKQ: Is hardcore where someone like, is getting hurt? And if so, is a stuffed animal a someone? [*presses finger into steam on window*] What do you mean? I need you to clarify.

QNNQR: You masturbate to pornography where stuffed animals get hurt?

KWWKQ: [*draws smiley-face in steam*] Yeah why.

QNNQR: How do you know they're getting hurt?

KWWKQ pauses and looks at the smashed fry.

KWWKQ: I guess I just assumed so from the way they were getting hit. But to answer your question, about three times, no more—otherwise I get too sleepy to function like a normal human being [*laughs, sarcastic*] And there is so much I want to accomplish I just can't waste any of my time.

QNNQR: [*looks at smashed fry*] Oh me too. Sometimes I want to be a really good human and help everyone out. But then I always get this feeling like it would much more fun to try and hurt everyone. And I never feel the same thing for too long. It makes me really uncomfortable and I want to scratch my gums and face until I pass out. Every sleeping human is perfect and every person watching another human sleep knows it will never be that perfect.

A small child climbs on a booth across the room. KWWKQ watches. Then he flicks another fry. A fast food employee calls the number of their order and KWWKQ gets the food.

KWWKQ: Hey [*setting the food down*] Hey do you need some plastic silverware? They got a huge pile of plastic silverware in there by the back door man [*looks side to side*] you want some? It's there. I'm thinking about grabbing some. You know [*slowly*] for eating food with [*sips his drink*] at home.

QNNQR: No thanks. I have enough silverware. Having silverware and possessions makes me feel upset because there is proof that I am alive and I have things to maintain. I can't take care of plastic silverware right now [*slouches in booth*] I'm not prepared. Thanks though.

QNNQR looks at the smashed fry. KWWKQ looks too. It is hard not to look at the smashed fry. The homeless man sitting at the table next to them begins to yell, head against the table and arms spread gripping the edges. Then quiet.

KWWKQ: Let me know if you change your mind about the plastic silverware [*puts his drink to his face then takes it down quickly*] How about we do this: If you want some plastic silverware, just be like, 'It seems we've come to a fork in the road.' But don't make eye contact.

QNNQR: [*sips drink*] That's the signal? Ok. I'll say that, if I decide I want you to steal some plastic silverware for me.

KWWKQ: Great [*pause*] Hey guess what.

QNNQR draws a smiley face on the window steam, eating. Across the parking lot, the giant inflatable gorilla stares at them.

QNNQR: What.

KWWKQ: I can't get hard [*chewing*] I was lying before [*stares at smiley face*] When we were in grade school together, the third grade teacher would never let me go to the bathroom. I would get hard to keep the piss in me [*each word equally*] It really hurt. I could never concentrate. Every day I held it in [*swallows, pokes straw deeper*] Now I can't get hard.

QNNQR crosses out the smiley face, using his forefinger. The homeless man yells a few times. Is then quiet.

QNNQR: I value you less as a friend now. You know that. And so does the inflatable gorilla. Look how mad he is.

KWWKQ: [*not listening*] I got hard just keeping the piss back. I got hard to keep the piss inside me. But I ended up ruining my pants so many times. It was embarrassing having to put the seat up at the end of the day when people lined up to leave the classroom. I hate everything in the world. Catholic school taught me how to hate everything in the world. And they did a good job. I can't get hard anymore and I hate myself real-good.

QNNQR: Were you more of a hide the boner in your beltline kind of guy, or did you do the hunchback walk to hide it?

KWWKQ doesn't answer. At the table next to them, the homeless man is asleep. He is not yelling anymore. QNNQR and KWWKQ take turns drawing smiley faces in the window fog, only to erase them then wait for new fog. They finish their food without talking. They leave to the alley and share a cigarette. On the way out KWWKQ takes a huge handful of plastic utensils from by the backdoor.

QNNQR: [*knocking cigarette pack against thigh*] When we were inside I caught a guy looking at me and, I felt like I wanted to kill him [*taking plastic off cigarette pack*] Did you see that guy? With the sweater? [*vague gesture*] Of course, when I remembered about the laws against that, I decided not to do it. Otherwise I would have. It angers me that I have to not-kill him. He kept looking at me. I mean it was bullshit. That bothers me [*lights cigarette using his coat to block the wind*] Seriously. Let's kill him. Yeah, let's do this. Let's finish this cigarette then go kill him and then we can look at that smashed fry some more. Did you see that thing? I couldn't stop looking at it.

In the alley where they stand, only the head of the inflatable gorilla is visible from over the top of a garage.

QNNQR: The gorilla wants us to kill him.

KWWKQ: No, I don't want to kill him. I'm too weak. I don't want to kill him. Fighting makes me sick. I hate it. My dad punched my mom in the mouth one night and then made her sing happy birthday to him. And she couldn't sing it right. She kept trying. I tried to help her sing but my dad punched me in the mouth too and it hurt really bad. Then he did that every night after that. I had to fill my mouth will ice cubes to stop the hurting. But I don't think the hurting went away, I think it went to sleep. When something is sleeping, it will always come back. Barely anything is smart enough to die in its sleep. I held in so much piss when I was younger. So much. There is a lot. It is the size of the Atlantic but it is inside me. I think bigger things can be inside smaller things.

QNNQR: So we're not killing the sweater-guy who looked at me weird then kept looking at me? Yes or no. Just tell me.

KWWKQ: [*not listening, watching puddle*] I'm remembering the sound of the punch to my mom's face. She is the one who taught me how to forget things. There is nothing as upsetting as the sound of a fist on someone's face. It's sick [*hits fist into hand*] Just beating flesh. Whap [*shivers*] Whap. Beating [*he stops, recalling something]* Hey, remember TYYTE? He was in our class. Really quiet guy—did you know him? It's hard to remember anyone else in our class. I never see them anymore. People are disappearing from my life. They don't announce it either.

QNNQR stares blankly. He looks down the alley in the direction of the parking lot. He vaguely offers the cigarette pack to KWWKQ, divided between appearing uncomfortable and appearing to care.

KWWKQ: He had glasses and black hair combed like, straight down—remember him? Really big eyebrows? [*moving on*] He's gone too [*toneless, slow*] They are all going to be gone.

QNNQR: [*offers cigarette pack*] He's gone?

KWWKQ: Yeah he's in jail now [*each word equally*] For life. He will die in a small concrete room [*takes cigarette*] That makes me want to laugh, but for some reason I can't actually do it. I can't laugh right now [*lights cigarette*] I thought I was going to but I can't. Fuck. I'm going to keep trying I think.

QNNQR exhales slowly and kicks a stone into a puddle. He looks up at the head of the inflatable gorilla.

KWWKQ: He fucking beat some kid to death. TYYTE did. He was at the park just walking around and some kids yelled at him. Remember, he walked kind of weird? Remember that?

QNNQR: [*crunching rocks with shoe*] Yeah I do. Like a duck.

KWWKQ: You remember like a duck?

QNNQR: [*looks at KWWKQ*] No, I remember he walked like a duck. Unless, do ducks remember the same way as we do or what? Sorry man, I'm trying not to look at the gorilla. It's fucking scary for some reason.

KWWKQ: Yeah [*looks at half cigarette, then tosses it into the puddle by his feet, a hiss*] he was walking through the park, and there was a group of kids there. He walked through their game of Frisbee or whatever and one of the kids yelled something at him. TYYTE kept walking and then the kid threw the Frisbee at him. The Frisbee hit TYYTE in the head and—I guess—he just turned and ran at the kid. And beat him to death in front of his friends. Just knocked him out and then started slamming his head against a bench. The kid's friends didn't do anything. They were probably shocked or whatever. They probably felt weak and stupid. I guess. I guess they felt weak and stupid. They watched TYYTE pounding this kid's head into the bench until he died. I heard from one of the kid's friends that when TYYTE was beating the kid, that the kid's head actually like, cracked open and they could see his fucking brain. They could see his fucking brain I guess. They didn't put that in the paper, the part about the brains coming out of the broken skull. And then, TYYTE just sat there until the police came. He didn't do anything. He just sat there. He had on a Ghostbusters shirt, and there was blood all over it. I read that in the paper. And he just sat on the bench, the kid's dead body right near his feet. He just put his bloody hands at his sides and waited for the police. And that was that [*pause*] I bet TYYTE held in a lot of piss too.

A lot. There is a lot of piss. There is an amount that is bigger than the earth inside the earth. There is an amount that is bigger than a human inside each human.

He takes another cigarette when offered. As he lights it he realizes he has lit the filter. Tosses it to the ground. Both men are quiet for awhile. They watch cars pass by on the street across from the alley. Too fast to make out faces. QNNQR looks at the inflatable gorilla again.

QNNQR: [*toneless*] Beating flesh.

KWWKQ: [*still watching cars*] Even though TYYTE is a murderer, I think he was my friend. I consider him my friend. I remember he helped me clean up my piss after school once. I would wait until everyone left the classroom at the end of the day to put up my seat because there was always piss pooled on my seat. And I didn't want people to see it run off onto the floor. So I'd wait until everyone left the room. Then like, TYYTE stayed after to try to catch a bee that was in the room, I think. When he saw my piss falling off the table he cleaned it up with his backpack and left quickly. Then he kept helping me. Every day. Every day he would help me. So I had him over once because I felt bad for him. It was awkward at first. He didn't say anything. I kept calling him retarded. I kept punching him in the temple and calling him retarded. He just kept staring at me. Then he started calling me retarded [*taps toe in puddle*] We were drinking juice boxes in the basement and he saw the glass cages I had on the counter. I had like two or three glass cages on the counter in the basement where I'd keep spiders that I'd caught. I'd catch spiders and put them in, and they'd make webs—it was nice to watch—that's why I did it. And I liked to come home to the spiders because I knew something was waiting for me. It was nice to talk to someone after pissing in my pants every day. Staring at the teacher with a hard dick, pissing on myself [*shakes head*] I didn't like that.

A car drives by, in slow bumps through the alley. QNNQR tries to look through the windshield but the windshield is black and he can't see the driver. He returns to staring at the gorilla.

QNNQR: I don't know what's going on.

KWWKQ: [*watching car drive away*] I loved the spiders. After they'd build their webs, I'd grab like an ant or some other bug from the basement floor and toss it into the web. Then I'd rescue it right before it was going to be killed and let it go.

QNNQR: [*puts hands in coat pockets*] You are so considerate. You are the ant savior.

KWWKQ: Helping them made me excited. The excitement made me want to hurt myself [*pauses*] I used to breed the spiders too. I would put a bunch of spiders together and they made more. That felt good to me. When TYYTE was over he kept staring at the cages. He got all excited. Started asking questions. I got tired of answering his questions, so I decided to show him the bee-trick. He liked bees.

QNNQR: The bee-trick?

KWWKQ nods his head and spits into the puddle by his feet, taps the puddle with a toe. The white spit moves to the center of the puddle and floats.

KWWKQ: Fuck [*wipes spit off mouth with sleeve*] Yeah, the bee-trick—you know?—if you catch a bee and put it in the freezer?—you don't know this?

QNNQR is staring at the spit in the puddle. He taps the formative ice fringe on the puddle and breaks it down.

QNNQR: No. I don't know it.

KWWKQ: If you catch a bee and then put it in the freezer, it gets paralyzed and kind of dies—but you can tie a little string around it while it's paralyzed and then when it thaws out you can walk around with it like a kite.

QNNQR: I am thinking you were a sad child.

KWWKQ: [*ignores*] When I told TYYTE about it he asked me to show him. I fucking had to show him. We caught a bee and put it in the freezer. He kept asking me, 'Are you sure it's not gonna die? Are you sure it's not gonna die?' He looked really worried. It was weird. I told him that this was how we controlled everything that God made. I told him to pay attention. So we eventually get the string on the bee and TYYTE is standing over it on the counter. He had his face like an inch away from it. Then he yells, 'It's moving, it's moving.' Starts laughing and pinching his crotch. We went outside and walked around with the bee until it died like, an hour later. A kite is something you can't really control. That was the only time I ever saw TYYTE smile. What an asshole. Just walking around the backyard holding a string with a bee on the end of it. I resent everyone. Sharing memories is the worst way to live. Sharing memories with someone else is terrible. Sharing memories is a kite. My entire life. Fuck everything that I can see and even the things that have yet to become. People are disappearing from my life. And they don't announce it. Not sharing memories with someone else is the only way to lose them.

They are silent. They stare at the gorilla. The air is late afternoon blue. They walk across the street, one after the other, to KWWKQ's truck.

KWWKQ: A kite is something you can't really control.

QNNQR: I agree.

KWWKQ: [*opening door*] You can still have some of that plastic silverware if you want it. I have a lot of it [*taps pocket*] Just ask if you want it. Just let me know.

They get in KWWKQ'S truck and drive away creaking. A train passes parallel to them as they drive. QNNQR watches the train pass next to him. Then it is gone. Quiet except for the creaking, again. They have nowhere to be. KWWKQ drives around and after many blocks they end up at a cemetery. It is dark out now.

KWWKQ: [*pulling in slowly*] Hey I think she's buried back here [*turns off headlights*] I fucking hated her man. I felt real hate for her. And I'm not sorry or looking to change. I am myself right now. And I fucking hated her man.

QNNQR puts his arm in the area between window track and rolls up the window.

QNNQR: Who?

KWWKQ: [*head out window, searching*] The teacher who would never let me piss. She's buried back here.

QNNQR clears his throat, an attempt at distance.

QNNQR: We should piss on her grave [*looks ahead through the windshield trying to remember what he just said but it's impossible*] I'm just saying [*pauses*] What did I say again?

KWWKQ: [*turning*] Fuck. I'll do it. Yeah I'll definitely do it. I want to piss on her dead face. I'll totally do that. I want her to taste it [*laughs*] I want to prove that I'm not sorry [*then firmly*] I'm not sorry man.

They drive around the cemetery path slowly, headlighting different graves. Eventually they find the one they want.

KWWKQ: Here [*parks truck*] you watch the truck while I go piss on her grave.

QNNQR: What happens if I don't watch the truck? I want to come with.

KWWKQ: It will run away. It will be gone. That's what will happen. Just stay here.

KWWKQ gets out and walks to the grave. QNNQR sits in the idling truck. He sees a leaf on the hood of the truck, pinned by the windshield wipers. He wonders if that leaf will be there for long or not really long at all. He wonders if the fry is still smashed against the ground in the same place. And he wonders how long everything will be where it is, if anything will ever change, or if no change would be better.

KWWKQ: [*getting back into the truck*] I pissed right on the center so if it makes it through the dirt it will touch her dead face. 100% yay for me. You know?

QNNQR: It's not going to make it through the coffin.

KWWKQ: [*putting truck into gear, hitting headlights*] I promise it will make it through.

QNNQR: Well [*tapping the door with his arm and still looking at the leaf*] Good. Good job. You've accomplished your goal. I'm proud of you. You taught me how to defile a grave. There is no way for me to repay you but with a little smile that I will perform right now. Ready?

KWWKQ: [*pulls truck away*] I know [*laughs*] I really feel like I did something.

QNNQR: You didn't acknowledge my smile [*rests head back on headrest*] Now I feel worthless. But that will change in a few seconds when I forget why. No one knows how to keep anyone else company. That is true. But I love to waste time [*turns to KWWKQ*] Hey [*pats shoulder*] good work today.

They drive without speaking. They look around to see if anything has become different about the world and maybe they just haven't noticed. They decide everything will always look the same, and that that is not comforting. And TYYTE is waiting on the bench with blood all over his shirt. He is walking around with a string tied to the dead kid's neck, the dead kid floating. He is with his two friends, driving without a place to be. Reminding them how everyone is pretty much in one place—that there really is only one place and that there are just basically dividers in the form of walls and water and roads and other things like that. They return to the fast food place and sit in the same booth and look at the same smashed fry.

KWWKQ: [*laughing*] I brought my own silverware [*looks at where the smiley face was, stops laughing*] And I am still full of the same piss.

QNNQR draws another smiley face.

QNNQR: A kite is something you can't control.

KWWKQ: I know.

QNNQR repeats the phrase "a kite is something you can't control" over and over and they look at the smashed fry until an employee tells them the restaurant is closing.

THE PEDOPHILE (AND HIS MENSES)

The gravel shoulder of a road surrounded by a forest preserve. A speed limit sign, a metal garbage can, and a portable toilet. The door to the portable toilet opens, and a pedophile exits. He wears a dirty all-gray sweatsuit, and a garbagebag mask over his head, eyeholes removed. He takes off the garbagebag and scratches his head. He looks at his fingers.

THE PEDOPHILE: [*shaking lice off fingertips*] They are still with me.

The pedophile walks into the forest preserve off to one side of the road. And he comes to a clearing. In the clearing there is dead grass and a picnic table and a boy, banging plastic trucks together and sitting alone. The pedophile stands back, watching.

THE PEDOPHILE: [*to himself*] They are still with me.

The pedophile puts the garbagebag mask back on. He walks into the clearing.

THE PEDOPHILE: [*whistles*] Hey, little man. You dropped this.

The pedophile reaches into his pocket, throws a bloody tampon at the boy. The tampon lands on the grass next to the boy's knees. Little pieces of leaf stick to it. And the boy looks at the tampon then back up at the pedophile.

THE BOY: That's not mine. I don't know what that is.

THE PEDOPHILE: [*insistent*] That is yours. I think you just don't recognize it. Maybe you don't remember dropping it. Maybe that's it.

The boy looks down at the tampon then back at the pedophile.

THE BOY: Maybe that's it.

THE PEDOPHILE: There it is, look at it [*pointing*] Come on now. You look at it. Look at it. Don't you like it? [*nodding*] You love it. You should have been blood.

The boy looks at the tampon. He is quiet. When he looks up at the pedophile, the pedophile's head covers the sun. All the boy sees is a black head circled by the sun. He shivers against it.

THE PEDOPHILE: Yes [*pause*] I am the eclipse [*pause*] Do you see me? [*pause*] Do you worship me?

THE BOY: [*coughs*] I feel cold. What're you doing to me?

THE PEDOPHILE: [*lifts hands, palms towards boy*] I'm not doing anything. You should move away from me if you are cold [*puts palms to the sky*] Everything in front of me gets dead. I hide everything in front of me. Do you worship me or not? Do you want to kiss me or not?

THE BOY: I don't know how to do that. I'm scared.

THE PEDOPHILE: [*puts hands down*] Everything is fine. Don't worry. You'll be fine. I don't want you to be scared. Everything is fine. I hide the things in front of me. And you are one of them [*evenly*] You are going to die too. You know that right? It might take you longer than me, but you will get there, I believe in you. I believe in you. I do. Do you believe in me?

THE BOY: [*looking at tampon*] Thank you for believing in me.

The boy pinches the tampon; it leaves some maroon-colored blood on his fingers. He wipes his fingers on the grass then smells them. He retches.

THE PEDOPHILE: [*laughing*] Do you smell something nice? Do you smell something you remember? [*evenly*] You should've been that. You should've been blood. I have you all over my fingers. You are still with me.

The pedophile leaves the clearing, returns to the woods. The boy smells his fingers again. He retches.

ALL THE DISCIPLES

A partially-filled bus, moving. Near the front, an old man sits behind the driver. The old man adjusts the Velcro on his shoes. He looks through the windshield. In the distance, miles away, there is a giant fire that is black, red, and white static. The fire that is black, red, and white static covers the rest of the earth. The bus drives towards the giant fire. And even if the bus stopped, it would still be moving towards the fire.

OLD MAN IN VELCRO SHOES: [*still looking through windshield*] When I got on the bus, I watched my footprints in the snow, behind me, connecting the doorway of my apartment with the steps of this bus. They got smaller and smaller—and now I can't see them. That means they are gone. My apartment building is behind me. I can't see my footprints in the snow. They're gone [*taps foot in runoff in aisle*] I can't tell if I miss them. Not yet.

BUS DRIVER: [*biting thumbnail*] Good story [*pulls to a slow stop at a streetlight*] Check it out.

The bus driver holds the front of his sweatshirt out flat. There is a cartoon cat on the front. Its arms are folded and beneath it are the words, "Not Impressed."

BUS DRIVER: Man, this cat is pissed, am I right? [*smiles and looks back and forth between the old man's mouth and eyes*] What do you think? Pissed or no?

OLD MAN IN VELCRO SHOES: [*watching the fire through the windshield*] Yeah, I think it is, I think you're right.

BUS DRIVER: [*looks at sweatshirt, chin down*] You bet it is. I mean look how it has its arms folded [*points*] Plus it has its tongue out, see that? Totally pissed.

OLD MAN IN VELCRO SHOES: I see that [*pointing*] The light's green.

The bus pulls off. A middle-aged man gets on at a stop and sits up front. At another stoplight, the bus driver attempts to show the middle-aged man the pissed-off cat but the middle-aged man cuts him off and points to the green light. And the bus driver pulls the bus over, idles. He touches his face with his hands. He cries and everyone on the bus looks at the fire that is black, red, and white static. They are closer now, idling. When someone in the back yells about "getting going," the bus driver slowly lifts his head, turns and stares blankly at the rest of the bus, face raw with tears. Then he pulls out onto the street again. The bus continues on towards the giant fire that is black, red, and white static.

[*Later on.*]

BUS DRIVER: [*to no one in particular*] I just realized, like yesterday, that all I do is drive around the edge of the town. That's it. I never leave. Never. Sometimes I think about coming up with something, some kind of reason to leave. Like I'll say, maybe I need to go to that miniature golf place, the one across the bridge [*clears throat*] but I don't. I never actually have to go miniature golfing [*clears throat again*] I just want to sleep in my closet but I have to come do this every day. I never leave [*pauses*] Today, we are going to leave.

There is no talking for a while. The bus creaks.

SOMEONE IN THE BACK: [*for everyone to hear*] All the disciples are inferior retard life.

At the next stop someone gets up and descends the stairs.

BUS DRIVER: [*to the person*] Hey wait.

Person turns.

BUS DRIVER: Name something you did that you think was great.

PERSON: Uh [*thinks for a moment*] I actually flushed my toilet this morning after shitting in it. And I saw all the disciples.

BUS DRIVER: The disciples are all inferior retard life.

PERSON: Yeah I made them gone.

BUS DRIVER: So you thought that was great?

PERSON: Yes and everything else about me too [*nodding*] Pretty much everything.

BUS DRIVER: [*pulls his sweatshirt flat, then loudly*] Not impressed.

PERSON: Ok. Bye. I will never see you again.

BUS DRIVER: No. You won't [*turns to windshield again*] Not impressed. Bye.

The person leaves. Other people sit in the back and on the sides of the bus. One of them is taking out a cellular phone.

PERSON WITH PHONE: [*to the woman next to him*] No I'm telling you. I know other people [*holds phone out*] Here, listen [*plays message*]

THE MESSAGE: [*female voice*] Heyyyeee [*pause*] Just calling to see what's up [*pause*] ouch—hit my toe [*breathing*] How's everything? I have work until eight. Oh man, yeah, there's this guy at the pet store here—he looks like, hmmm [*static-cracking of phone adjustment*] he looks like Abe Lincoln or some shit [*pause*] Uh so, call me when you get a chance. I wanted to see what you're doing tonight. Maybe you want to hang out [*pause*] Huh, looks like Abe Lincoln Guy wants a goldfish. He should buy at least two if he's going to do it so they're not lonely. Sometimes people tell me the fish just stop eating when they're alone. Just, ploop, dead [*pause*] ploop. It takes a goldfish a long time to die for some reason. Ploop. There were some here that just floated sideways for days and days. Ploop. Come on Abe Lincoln Guy, you know you want two—no, don't put your hand in the tank, ewww his hands are really hairy—God, the hairs are like, floating. I'm fucking bored, oh shit, who'm I talking to? [*pause*] Oh yeah, hey, call me whenever you get a chance [*long exhalation*] on my lunchbreak today I tried disappearing beneath a big piece of broken blacktop in the parking lot but I only managed to get part of my head underneath and the rest of the time I spent digging up little pieces of the grass out front of the store and burying my phone or blaming the ripped-up grass on birds, as customers walked in. Ploop. I looked up at the sky like I know I lost something there but I couldn't remember what to look for. I was jealous that I lost it and it didn't lose me. The sky looks like a wonderful place and I am high on being away from you. Don't call me. Ploop. My apartment will be quiet when I get home. Ploop. Today I'll get tired. Every human has getting tired in common. There. I feel so compassionate. I'll go to my room and lay on my bed. And I won't be upset. Don't call me. I could understand a god that created me and now doesn't like me, and maybe hates me. And creates other things that hate me too. And for me to hate. I can see making a mistake too. Ploop—

The message cuts her off while she is still talking. The bus moves towards the giant fire that is black, red, and white static. The bus becomes warm.

[*Later.*]

A small child and his mother sit together in the back. Near them sits a 20-year-old man. The small child is playing a video game. He looks up for a second then back at the game.

20 YEAR-OLD MAN: [*to the child*] Hey.

The child doesn't respond. And the mother isn't paying attention either. She's staring at the fire, her face calm.

20 YEAR-OLD MAN: What are you playing?

CHILD: [*eyes down*] Mario.

20 YEAR-OLD MAN: Nice.

CHILD: [*looks up quickly*] Yeah, I'm trying to get past the third world.

20 YEAR-OLD MAN: [*puts arms over back of seat, crosses legs*] Oh yeah?

CHILD: Yeah. It's hard—[*licks some snot from top lip*] I need more points.

20 YEAR-OLD MAN: [*looks at fire then back at the child*] Why do you need points?

The child shrugs his shoulders.

20 YEAR-OLD MAN: What do you mean? [*mimics shrugging*]

CHILD: I need points to get another life.

20 YEAR-OLD MAN: Why do you want another life?

CHILD: [*shrugs again*] To beat the world.

20 YEAR-OLD MAN: For what?

CHILD: For more points.

20 YEAR-OLD MAN: Why?

Pause.

CHILD: For another life.

20 YEAR-OLD MAN: So if you died right now? [*folds hands on lap*] You wouldn't have that extra life, would you? [*looks at fire*]

CHILD: Nope [*accidentally kicks man's shin*] Sorry.

20 YEAR-OLD MAN: That's fine. So, you wouldn't get the life and you wouldn't beat the world?

CHILD: [*tongue on upper-lip again*] Nope.

20 YEAR-OLD MAN: And then no points.

CHILD: Yup.

20 YEAR-OLD MAN: That sounds pointless [*quickly*] But good luck.

The 20-year-old man turns and stares through his window. The phrase "now what" repeats in his mind. On someone's front lawn he sees a snowman—half-melted with a crow on its head. The snowman looks unhappy. It is going to die soon. Another set of roads opens up. Over and over. They are getting closer to the fire.

20-YEAR-OLD MAN: Now what.

THE MOTHER: [*to his back*] You feel free because the thing that encircles you is so big you can't see it.

The 20-year-old man says nothing, just looks out his window.

[*Later.*]

Front of the bus again. There is fog on the windshield. The bus driver wipes off the windshield with his sleeve and surveys the road. Behind him, an old woman sits next to a fat bald man.

OLD WOMAN: [*looking from fogged windshield to the fat bald man*] It's supposed to be cold out all this week.

FAT BALD MAN: [*turning to her, nodding*] Yeah—yes it is. Every year, the earth rotates and sometimes it's farther from the sun. That makes it cold. It will happen again next year too. Just so you know. Also, the white accumulations are something called snow, but that's too much for our current lecture. We'll cover snow tomorrow.

OLD WOMAN: [*straightening a wrinkle on her pants*] My grandson is coming over this afternoon and I wanted to take him outside, but I think it's too cold. He loves it outside though. He definitely loves it [*shrugs, smiling*] I don't love anything. But he loves the outside.

She reaches into her purple corduroy purse and holds out a Polaroid.

OLD WOMAN: That's him holding a balloon [*points*] I like how the sun makes his hair look like ice. He's in preschool now. Preschool is where you begin to learn that no one will ever like you.

FAT BALD MAN: [*nodding, still looking at the picture*] Balloons die.

They turn away from each other. The water from their boots drips into the grooves of the aisle. And silence fits the bus in a swell.

OLD WOMAN: [*looking out the window at the static fire*] I am becoming a terrible scab [*coughs, covers her mouth with the hand holding the picture*] This is unbearable. I miss him. I miss him so much.

She stares at the picture with her watery eyes. Tries to wipe off the streaks from her cough.

FAT BALD MAN: [*pointing to a boy sitting next to her the whole time*] Is that your grandson? I think he's right next to you.

OLD WOMAN: [*still looking at picture*] Yes. I'm going to miss him. I brought the picture so nothing would be left behind. Wherever you go you have to remember everything you take with.

The grandson climbs up the old woman and puts his mittens against her ear, says something. She looks down by her feet intently, then smiles at him.

OLD WOMAN: I do remember. I do.

He smiles and she lifts him onto her lap.

OLD WOMAN: And do you remember what he says?

FAT BALD MAN: [*intervening*] What who says?

The grandson looks at the fat bald man then shrinks in embarrassment. He ducks beneath the old woman and searches the fat bald man through the coat's armpit.

OLD WOMAN: [*nodding*] Actually, a parrot.

The grandson puts his whole head out through the armpit, and the fat bald man watches two small lips.

THE GRANDSON: A sad parrot.

OLD WOMAN: Yes, a sad parrot [*smiles*] Whenever we walk by this one pet shop, there's always this parrot in a cage in the window—and my grandson thinks he looks sad.

THE GRANDSON: [*head out through her armpit*] Yeah, he's the saddest parrot ever.

OLD WOMAN: And what does he say?

THE GRANDSON: [*straightens up and smiles*] He says, 'Quaaa-aaaawwwww.' He's super sad.

FAT BALD MAN: [*smiles*] Quaaaa-aaaaawwww. Is it like that?

BUS DRIVER: [*turns*] How do we actually know the parrot's sad? What if that's his happy quaaw? Or his "maybe I'm uncertain about the future" quaaw.

The old woman says nothing. The grandson says nothing.

FAT BALD MAN: Quaaaawwwwwwww—quawww.

Someone in the back quaws too. The whole bus begins to quaw. Then there is abrupt quiet.

FAT BALD MAN: [*looking at the grandson but addressing the old woman*] Do you still want him. Do you want him to be yours? I mean he looks fine and everything. Nothing seems to be wrong with him.

OLD WOMAN: Yes I want him. I brought the picture with so no one else could have it. He is my lamb. He is a talking collection of my blood surrounded by skin that I recognize and love. And I am taking him with.

FAT BALD MAN: [*breathing heavily*] If he is your lamb then [*stops, tries to control labored breathing*] I can't take him away from you [*looking at floor*] Fuck, I feel shitty [*looks at fire, rubbing forehead, then he vomits into the aisle*] Oh shit.

The bus reeks rotten vegetable scent.

OLD WOMAN: [*moving her feet from the vomit*] Thank you for not taking my lamb.

FAT BALD MAN: [*wipes mouth, shivers*] Take good care of your lamb.

OLD WOMAN: I will.

Trees shake outside and garbage skips over the ground. The fire is closer, stands higher. Across the aisle a man stands holding the metal pole with one hand and reading a newspaper with the other hand. Sitting next to him there's a girl with 47 chromosomes. She has a very small head. Her eyes are crossed and magnified by her glasses. She drools over her chin. She swings her legs over the seat, licking her mouth. She wears purple boots. They look fake, like boots from a doll. She hits them together and looks around, swinging her lunchbox. Next to her, a sleeping man wakes when his head hits his knee after a bump. He looks out the window at the giant fire in the distance.

SLEEPING MAN: [*weary, smiling at the girl with 47 chromosomes*] We will be there soon. We are on track. I am sleeping so the wait seems shorter.

The girl with 47 chromosomes smiles and addresses him.

GIRL WITH 47 CHROMOSOMES: [*showing the sleeping man her lunchbox*] I yike ponies. I yikedum ayot.

SLEEPING MAN: I see. That's wonderful. It's good that you have them on your lunchbox then. Right?

He rests his head again and the girl with 47 chromosomes continues her conversation with the man standing in the aisle holding a support pole.

GIRL WITH 47 CHROMOSOMES: I yike ponies ayot [*laughs and puts her fingers in her mouth*] Ponies aw good.

The girl with 47 chromosomes hits her pony lunchbox against the metal pole in the aisle. She laughs and drool pulses out around her fingers, lands on her lap. There is sweat on her face and neck.

MAN STANDING IN AISLE: Me too. Ponies are great. Ponies are those things that make webs and have eight legs right? Is that what I'm thinking of?

The girl with 47 chromosomes smiles and kicks her boots together, flinging melted snow across the aisle.

GIRL WITH 47 CHROMOSOMES: I yikedum ayot.

MAN STANDING IN AISLE: Well good. I'll have to buy a lunchbox with them on it. Because of how good they are.

The bus stops and more people get on. A bird flies in with them and lands on a seat. It looks around in quick twitches. Then the bird intones a high-pitched humming that nauseates everyone. They all touch at their temples with their fingertips. Many of them cringe and vomit. Others scream.

GIRL WITH 47 CHROMOSOMES; [*tensing with excitement*] Burrdy [*laughs*] Burrdy.

The bird flies to the front of the bus. The humming stops. Then starts. Alternates at random.

BUS DRIVER: [*stares at bird, then back and forth from bird to windshield*] When I was like six—I found a baby bird on the sidewalk. My mom had taken me to the zoo. It looked like you—[*laughs, addresses bird*] just like you. It'd fallen from the nest and died I guess, it was all bald and gnarled up [*looks out windshield*] And when I kicked the bird with my tennis shoe, the bird scraped along the sidewalk—it was all stiff—it was just a shell. Some ants walked out of its mouth. The ants ate it from the inside I guess [*pauses, turns to bird again*] There must be ants in me too. I don't have faith in anything. I am the saddest bastard ever [*smiles*] It makes me sad that a woman gave birth to me so I could drive a bus and then go home and sit on my couch watching tv in order to have something to talk about with other people. The ants are always so hungry. It is impossible to get rid of them. I can't get rid of them. I don't know when they came, but the ants are with me. The ants are still with me you know? I was sad and confused that the bird was all-alone. But I will keep you company this time [*reaches for the bird, bird flies, high-pitched humming resumes as the bird flies around the bus, panicking*]

GIRL WITH 47 CHROMOSOMES: [*reaching, still seated*] Burrdy.

MAN STANDING IN AISLE: [*puts his newspaper down*] They fall out of the nest when the mom is gone [*looks at the girl with 47 chromosomes*] Your mother pushed you though [*looks around to other people*] Hey can any of you help me with these jumbles? These things are fucking ridiculous. Is 'jargub' a word? It's like, a mineral right?

GIRL WITH 47 CHROMOSOMES: [*face wrinkles with confusion*] No mah-mee?

She stops kicking her boots. They drip.

BUS DRIVER: Who's talking to who here?

SLEEPING MAN: [*raising his head, squinting*] No mommy. You retarded bitch.

SOMEONE ELSE: No mommy.

They are all quiet. Driving. Very warm.

[*Later.*]

In the middle area of the bus there are some seats facing sideways. A daughter is showing her mom how to perform 'Stop, Drop and Roll.' She has just finished explaining 'Stop'.

THE MOM: [*clapping*] What's the second thing?

THE DAUGHTER: [*stops, slight tantrum with arms*] Stop, don't—I know it.

THE DAUGHTER *pauses, then drops to the floor.*

THE MOM: Sweetie, get off the floor.

THE DAUGHTER: [*protesting*] But that's the second thing.

The mom picks her daughter up and hugs her.

MAN SITTING ACROSS THE AISLE: [*watching*] Now you are both on fire. I'm imagining your girl covered in flames. Her My Little Ponies shirt drops in smoldering pieces—but she lives, because she will stop, drop and roll. I think maybe hugs put out fires too though. Maybe I'm wrong.

THE MOM: [*still hugging daughter*] After you learn to tie your shoes, you have to learn how to keep from dying. How to stay away from cars, killers, rapists, fires, and whatever else will kill you or change you. One of the things you learn at a young age is what to do when your body is on fire. You also learn how to hide from the weather, and bombs, and how to avoid free candy. You learn how to make pretty letters, how to count, and how to avoid getting hit by a car and/or getting hit by a car then raped—I am trying to remember if I learned that last one or not.

The man across the aisle nods.

BUS DRIVER: [*to no one*] I don't know, I feel weird but sometimes like, I'm looking at my kids, and I think "It's time to kill them now, all of them." When that happens I go to the garage and sit on the floor, next to the refrigerator. I like how it hums. It calms me down. I like how it hums. I take a big handful of ice out of the freezer, and then I sit on the garage floor and skip them across the ground. I like it.

The bird resumes the highpitch humming-squeal. In the distance, everything burns and leaks into space the same color. They drive towards the fire that is black, red, and white static.

BUS DRIVER: [*through p.a.*] Hello everyone. It's time to think about all the things we wish we had in our pockets to go with us.

The bus passes two women on a swingset in an abandoned school playground. One woman swings and one woman is unmoving. The two women watch the bus pass, sweating.

UNMOVING WOMAN: The fire is making my pores leak honey into my body. The heat is painful. Will you scrape open my pores so I can leak the honey out quicker? Will you do that?

MOVING WOMAN: [*looks over her shoulder on an upswing*] A million needles to hold you in place while I scrape you clean. You don't have to be worried. You just have to sit still.

UNMOVING WOMAN: [*laughing, still looking at fire*] You will never see me smile again [*stops laughing, looks grave*] Really though, I'm really scared. And I don't think you will ever see me smile again.

MOVING WOMAN: [*looking at the fire*] My face and body are getting warm. We will have to move soon.

Neither says anything.

CANCER KILLS [1]

A pizza delivery person stands at the front door of someone's house. He goes to knock again but then hears someone undoing the lock. A man opens the door.

PIZZA DELIVERY PERSON: Here you are sir. It's fourteen eighty-five.

MAN: [*taking the pizza*] Uh, ok. Hold on [*reaches for his wallet*] Uh, do you want to come in? You can come in if you want. I'll give you some of my pizza here and we can watch tv or something—whatever you like to do. I have board games.

PIZZA DELIVERY PERSON: [*stops chewing gum and squints at the man*] What?

MAN: Yeah. Come on in.

The pizza delivery person pops a bubble. Then he is quiet.

MAN: [*softly*] Please. Please stay. We can talk or I can make you laugh maybe. Come on–please? I'll pay you for the pizza but please stay.

PIZZA DELIVERY PERSON: No thanks sir. That's fourteen eighty-five, please.

MAN: [*clears his throat*] Isn't there anything I can do to get you to please please please stay even for ten minutes. It's so bad in there.

PIZZA DELIVERY PERSON: There is nothing you can do to get me to stay. Please pay sir [*then slowly*] There is nothing you can do to get me to stay—nothing.

MAN: [*looks at the pizza box*] That's what I thought.

THE BASTARDS
[THEY ERASE A WEAKLING]

Night. Snow. Three men are driving down a road that cuts through a forest preserve. They stop at red lights automatically, without recognizing any of them. They stop, and stare blinkless. Above them, the powerlines blink red blooms onto the forest in a slow rhythm. And they drive through it.

THE DRIVER: [*staring*] I believe that when you die, your skeleton pushes up through the dirt and becomes a tree. And I believe the tallest tree is the saddest because it has no friends—all it does is make those beneath it cold [*looks at the man in passenger seat*] You know?

A deer cuts across the road, diving into the bushes. They miss it. The person in the passenger seat has both hands to his face. His face is ripped from the corner of the left side of his mouth to his earlobe. It hangs open. There is blood down his neck, hard and becoming maroon along the collar of his shirt. He keeps clearing the blood out from his streaming sinuses to keep from choking.

THE MAN WITH THE RIPPED FACE: I always wondered if my face was a real thing, like a bunny, or, like a tree. Now I know. I know it is a real thing. Or a fake thing that can still hurt you.

He sits up, struggling. The blood leaks through his teeth.

THE DRIVER: [*ignores*] Just saying most people believe that when you die, you just go beneath some dirt. But I believe your skeleton pushes up through the dirt and becomes a tree. The tallest tree is the saddest because all it does is make the things below it cold [*turns to the man with the ripped face*] I believe all the things I just said.

THE MAN WITH THE RIPPED FACE: [*looking at his lap, pooled red*] I admit that I have been one of those people, who believes that when you die the skeleton just stays underground. I'll admit that—that has been me. I'll also admit that I've been repeating the things I see around me, to myself, to make sure I haven't died. But I'm willing to hear how this tree-thing happens too [*coughs, clears throat*] That seems interesting to me. Go on [*chokes, spits out some blood; it goes all over his lap*] I want to listen [*then pleading*] no, I don't want to be a tree yet. It's too cold out to become a tree. And I don't know any other trees so it will be hard to make friends [*looks around*] Did you clean your car recently? It looks nice.

Another man emerges from the lightlessness in the backseat, looking forward, a hand on each headrest.

THE MAN FROM THE LIGHTLESSNESS IN THE BACKSEAT: [*to the driver*] Where are we going? I don't feel good. Not like, I am sick, but something else. We should just pull over and leave him on the side of the road. We can even make a note. A nice note. A note that says, 'I love you, please help me if I'm not already dead.' We should leave him on the side of the road [*tapping headrests*] Yeah. I feel uncomfortable. Really uncomfortable now. I can smell him dying already. We have to kill him. Oh [*pause*] but, just to continue the debate earlier, I don't think you become a tree. I believe when you die, that's it. You don't have to say anything anymore, and you don't have to remember things, and you don't have to wake up, and you definitely don't have to be friends with anyone [*rubs hand on headrest*] Your car does look great; it smells like you vacuumed too. Be honest man, you vacuumed didn't you? It looks—honestly— like amazing. Fucking amazing.

THE DRIVER: [*staring forward, equal emphasis on each word*] I said no swearing in the car.

They stop at another stoplight, this one hung from a sagging wire. The car blooms red and remains red with the stoplight. All three stare at the red bulb. The area they are in now is a little darker but the procession of powerlines can still be seen far off, connecting nothing. The man with the ripped face bleeds down his neck.

THE DRIVER: [*still staring at the bulb*] When someone is bleeding, that is good, right. That means there is life. That means you are turning inside out [*looks at the man with the ripped face but addresses the man in the backseat*] I don't smell him dying yet. The blood that is coming out of his face smells good. I don't even mind that it is ruining my car. The car that, yes, I recently vacuumed. We should go somewhere where we can help him. Help him to fix his face. It looks all weird right? Maybe we can make his face normal again. Normal faces rule the world. You don't hear anything about ugly faces [*addressing the man with the ripped face*] You want to fix your face up? What should we do—it's up to you [*laughs*] That sounds like a song [*singing*] 'What should we do, it's up to you.' Alright let's go then [*drives off*] I have seen so many faces, it will be easy to make yours look similar [*slowly*] I promise I will do my best.

THE MAN FROM THE LIGHTLESSNESS IN THE BACKSEAT: [*looking out the back windshield at the red light of the powerlines*] We are professionals at creating believable human faces.

The road curves. They go further into the forest preserve. Redness from the powerlines alternates with the blackness of the woods.

THE MAN WITH THE RIPPED FACE: Yeah man [*swallowing, he convulses*] Yeah. Fix me. Don't leave me. Please don't kill me. You can fix me [*coughing all over*] Fuck [*he curls up*] Alright. Somebody tuck me in. Reach out the window and pull off some branches and sew them all together. I'm cold. I'm a hopeless adolescent. I haven't gone through puberty yet. I'm dying [*moans, hits head against window, repeatedly*] We don't have to figure out what happens to your skeleton, we just have to keep mine warm.

They turn and go down an even darker road. The man from the lightlessness in the backseat returns to the lightlessness. His face then only visible in red pulses. The woods sway black around them.

THE MAN FROM THE LIGHTLESSNESS IN THE BACKSEAT: Even though this car is moving, I know I am not. I am not moving at all, the car is moving [*pauses*] But it feels good to be out with other people now, you know? Even though one of them is dying and ruining the car. Thanks to both of you. I mean that. Sometimes I forget how much other people help me. How much they mean to me. I'm not even lying to you right now. I really like that you guys are here. I am trying to be less negative about life [*taps headrest with balled fist*] This is Step One right here.

THE DRIVER: [*nods to the man with the ripped face*] Hey check the glovebox and see if there's any gum in there. There should be a pack of gum in there. I just bought one.

The man with the ripped face opens the glovebox. He searches with one hand and holds the torn-cheek together with his other hand.

THE MAN WITH THE RIPPED FACE: My blood tastes thin. Like, it tastes so thin. It seems really thin in my mouth [*shuffling things in glovebox*] But I mean, I kind of like the way it tastes. Is that good or bad? I don't see the gum. Saying things out loud is a way to let other people think about them. Is that good or bad?

THE DRIVER: [*evenly*] We'll fix your face when you check for the gum.

THE MAN WITH THE RIPPED FACE: [*shuffles things around in the glovebox again*] Nah, there's [*clears nose*] there's only the empty pack and those little paper sleeve things.

THE DRIVER: [*eyes still forward, equal emphasis on each word*] What happened to it? Did you take a piece or two when I wasn't looking?

THE MAN WITH THE RIPPED FACE: I don't know. I really can't remember. Please help me. I can't take it. I really can't take it. Great, I just forgot my middle name. Do I even have a middle name? I am never going to be able to smile the same way again. There is no pain in that though [*his pale hand shaking over the wound*] But I do need help. Really.

THE MAN FROM THE LIGHTLESSNESS IN THE BACKSEAT: [*toneless*] You will do better in life if you don't smile. Something has already been fixed there. I promise that.

The driver turns off the headlights and drives, accessing a gravel road. All of the men then visible only when the powerlines go red.

THE DRIVER: [*firmly, to the man with the ripped face*] Maybe you should kill yourself if it hurts so bad. I'll start driving really fast and you can jump out of the car [*pointing for emphasis*] That—will kill you [*pause*] You are so selfish and greedy. Just like with the gum. The gum is proof. If it hurts so bad then do it, jump out and break your body on a tree. Then, thank me. No wait, thank me in advance [*clears throat and sits up straighter in seat*] Or, you can start writing the note, the one we leave on your body when we pull over and drop you off [*patting thigh of the man with the ripped face*] And be nice if you want someone to adopt you [*smiling*] Hey you can even write your little note with the paper sleeves left over from the gum you stole [*teasing*] You greedy greedy man. Anyway so, we've given you some options.

THE MAN FROM THE LIGHTLESSNESS IN THE BACKSEAT: [*leans forward*] And I'll watch out the back windshield to make sure it is real, when you hit the tree and die. We can bury you and water the ground where you are, so you become such a big big tree—the tallest [*taps shoulder of the man with the ripped face*] And I'm still offering to write the note. I'll start it off like, 'Dear sir or madam, please help me. I'm an orphan, and as you can see my face is ripped in half. I can't smile, but I'm smiling inside.'

THE DRIVER: [*puts both hands on the wheel, car slows—red light more intense, closer*] Oh, I definitely like that. We'll use that, I can't think of anything better than that. Good job.

They are quiet. The driver parks beneath a powerline and watches the person next to him hold his face together. In every pulse of red light they appear as red faces.

THE DRIVER: [*staring at the man with the ripped face*] Your face is all red. There is red all over it. Does that make it hurt more? Can you feel the red on your face? Is it heavy?

THE MAN WITH THE RIPPED FACE: [*panicked*] Huh? What is it? What's happening? [*points*] It's on you too. Can you feel it? What does it feel like? It's getting very heavy now [*touches face with both hands, looks at hands and wipes them off on seat*]

THE DRIVER: [*staring at powerlines, gesturing slowly*] It's just the lights [turns to *the man with the ripped face*] It's just the lights [*softly*] Another thing I believe is that the lights are all the ghosts of people you have known. It's just the lights. That's all it is.

THE MAN WITH THE RIPPED FACE: It feels like it's on me. Is it on me? Now I'm afraid. Afraid I'll be red forever [*squirms in seat*] It's too heavy.

The driver touches the red on his own face, with his fingertips, staring at the man with the ripped face.

THE DRIVER: [*calmly*] It's just the lights. They are the ghosts of the people you have known. A ghost is something someone told you that you still remember. It's just the lights right? [*laughs*]

The man with the ripped face is quiet. He brings a sleeve to his mouth and tries to dry his teeth.

THE MAN WITH THE RIPPED FACE: I don't want to think about ghosts.

THE DRIVER: Sorry. I know how you are [*grabs his shoulder*] Are you ok though? Tell me if you're not ok, my very special friend. Do you feel special today? You look really bad but you're just as special as ever. I mean that. If I had a chart of how special you have been to me, it would have to be a—a really big piece of paper [*points for emphasis*] That's how special [*toneless, staring at red powerline light*] We are making ghosts together.

THE MAN WITH THE RIPPED FACE: [*rubbing face slowly*] It feels like the red is on my face. Are you sure it's not on me? Please take it off [*louder*] Just take it off me now. Take it off and let's drive away. Just, I am so tired and I want to be tucked in. Take the red off my face [*screams*] Please.

The driver turns on the headlights. A deer walks through the bushes and stands in front of the car. It stands on its hindlegs. All of its skin is gone. The deer is just muscle. And up the abdomen runs a long laceration—no organs inside. Red light drapes the deer in pulses. All stare. Everything quiet.

THE DRIVER: [*looking at his hands on the steering wheel, red*] Answer me. Come on. Did you steal the gum? Be honest with me. Don't let sixty-eight cents divide us. Tell me, did you steal it?

The man with the ripped face nods. The deer is still facing them, unmoving. Then it returns to the woods, walking backwards with slow precision.

THE DRIVER: Alright [*nodding*] I appreciate the honesty. Thank you.

They pull back onto the road. The forest preserve goes miles wide on all ends, soundless. Slow red flashes.

THE DRIVER: I don't know why, but I don't listen to the radio anymore [*firmly*] I just can't do it [*looks in rearview*]

THE MAN FROM THE LIGHTLESSNESS IN THE BACKSEAT: [*coming into view in red flashes*] Me neither. When I hear commercials or really shitty songs I feel like all my nerve endings are becoming bruised and my testicles are withering [*seems to forget conversation*] I'm always worried that other people are trying to kill me. But I know that everyone else was put on the earth to become my own. Not for me to be theirs. I believe there are little pieces of myself everywhere.

THE DRIVER: Yeah?

THE MAN FROM THE LIGHTLESSNESS IN THE BACKSEAT: Yeah, and I have to cancel every piece I find, so I become smaller and smaller. Always incomplete.

THE MAN WITH THE RIPPED FACE: [*quietly*] And do you want to be too small to see? I don't understand [*coughs, moans*]

THE MAN FROM THE LIGHTLESSNESS IN THE BACKSEAT: I don't. I definitely don't. I never want to fully cancel-out. I want to continue getting smaller, never actually ending. Otherwise I'd have nothing to do. I'm here to kill everything. Never actually ending.

The man with the ripped face coughs and lets his head rest against the fogged window. He winces as the coughing undoes the formative scabs along the inside of his mouth, all the way to his ear. There is quiet. And they drive on, little bumps as they go deeper along the gravel road.

THE DRIVER: [*staring forward*] Humans and homes and trees all look the same to me.

THE MAN WITH THE RIPPED FACE: [*coughing*] My fucking face. Fuck. Can you two still see me? [*decidedly*] That's it. I'm dead. Can either of you see me? Just tell me. Talk to me please. Tell me please [*leans forward, rests forehead on the dash*] Fuck can we just keep talking. I don't want to hear the quiet. I believe that other people are the most important thing you can see, or hear. I do.

Blood taps between his legs into the wet floormat. He coughs. He groans after each cough. The driver looks over and sees the bottom row of teeth through the wound, lit green by the light of the dash clock.

THE DRIVER: No one's listening to you [*alternating between the road and the teeth*] Hey, hey now there is green light on your teeth. Does that hurt? The green ghosts in your mouth? You are green and red. You are my Christmas-friend. Does it hurt to be Christmas? You're my friend for always and always [*quietly*] A friend is important when you realize how terrible everything is without someone to talk to constantly. You are my Christmas gift. Friend, you are a gift.

THE MAN WITH THE RIPPED FACE: [*looking up*] I am the blood that dripped from the Virgin when she was shaking from birthing a waste. Cattle gives birth then sleeps in the barn. Merry Christmas.

The driver laughs. They all laugh. The driver puts his fingers into the passenger's ripped face and touches the bloody teeth. He keeps laughing.

THE MAN FROM THE LIGHTLESSNESS IN THE BACKSEAT: [*taps both their headrests*] I think we all just learned together.

THE DRIVER: Let us all be scared in quiet now.

Quiet and cold air. They drive on. Somewhere deep in the forest preserve, the driver pulls over again. There is a speed limit sign, a gravel shoulder, and a portable toilet on the side of the road. Next to the car, a big metal garbage can. Everything becomes visible in red flashes, timed.

THE DRIVER: [*both hands on steering wheel*] Oh wait. Forgot one. I have another belief. It is that all the humans on earth are here to hold the earth in place. Otherwise the earth would float up to the ceiling of space where there is no air and no friendship.

THE MAN WITH THE RIPPED FACE: Can we fix my face now? [*resting his forehead on the dashboard, breathing slow*] I've been a good boy. I will sit and be a good boy while you clean me. But you have to promise to clean me [*looking up, trying to smile*] If I leave the earth there is one less person to hold it here. Aren't you scared of the ceiling of space? It is where no one should be.

The driver exits the car and the others follow. The man with the ripped face sits on the hood while the other two wipe his face clean with a diaper they find in the garbage can. And they hold out their lighters in front of them to make sure they do the job complete. Bleeding soaks the diaper.

THE DRIVER: [*throwing the bloody-diaper into the darkness*] Hold on, I have to piss.

He walks out of sight, into some bushes.

THE MAN WITH THE RIPPED FACE: [*leaning against the car*] Do I still look pretty though? Please tell me. What are your thoughts on my prettiness? [*coughs, spits—holding his face*]

THE MAN FROM THE LIGHTLESSNESS IN THE BACKSEAT: You have never looked more beautiful. I would purchase a poster with your face on it and I would write to my diary how cute you are every night if that were a possibility.

THE MAN WITH THE RIPPED FACE: [*sullenly*] That is not a possibility. I don't remember having my photograph taken to then be made into a poster. But, I still accept your apology.

THE MAN FROM THE LIGHTLESSNESS IN THE BACKSEAT: I didn't apologize for anything you motherfucker.

A sound from the bushes. The driver returns.

THE DRIVER: [*breathing clouds*] I feel better now. Much better. Now there is no more filth inside my body. The filth tries to fill my body and I try to fill the earth. You two mean very much to me. And I appreciate it.

Then the driver slams the man with the ripped face against the car by the throat, pressing hard, strangling. The man from the lightlessness follows and they press their four hands in hard, strangling. The flaps from the ripped and screaming face bleed onto their hands as they strangle, teeth rows visible through the tearing.

THE DRIVER: [*turning, still strangling*] I can't understand him. He's speaking blood. I am feeling an emotion and I don't know what it is [*motions with head*] Hey, use your thumbs more.

THE MAN FROM THE LIGHTLESSNESS IN THE BACKSEAT: [*turning and wincing*] My fingers kind of hurt. Maybe that's the emotion.

THE DRIVER: Yeah, mine do too. Let's stop.

THE MAN FROM THE LIGHTLESSNESS IN THE BACKSEAT: You go first. I'm more of a follower.

They take their hands off and the body falls. The driver holds up his bloody fingers, then splays them.

THE DRIVER: Do my nails look nice? Like a pretty girl at prom?

THE MAN FROM THE LIGHTLESSNESS IN THE BACKSEAT: Yes [*kicking gravel shyly*] They do. Do you want to dance with me?

They laugh. The man from the lightlessness in the backseat lifts the body onto the window's track by the hair, neck down. The driver gets into the car.

THE DRIVER: Hmm. He is maybe dead or maybe almost there [*pauses, tapping his fingers on the steering wheel*] He was one of God's choices. He will make a nice tree and I will hang a wreath on him.

The driver rolls the window up on the man's neck. His neck breaks, and his face coughs wetly on the seat.

THE MAN FROM THE LIGHTLESSNESS IN THE BACKSEAT: [*to himself, noticing his stained shoes*] Shit, my shoes are ruined. What will protect my feet now? If not my shoes then what? Oh wait [*stoops and gives thumbs-up to the driver*] I think he's good.

The driver makes the "I can't hear you, sorry" gesture from inside.

THE MAN FROM THE LIGHTLESSNESS IN THE BACKSEAT: [*louder*] I said, I think he's good.

He walks around the car. Knocks on the driver's window.

THE MAN FROM THE LIGHTLESSNESS IN THE BACKSEAT: [*motioning to roll down the window*] I was just saying I think he's good.

THE DRIVER: Yeah [*looking at the body, slumped and oddly still*].

Yeah I think I know what you mean and I think so too. I think he's good. Sometimes when I am eating a candy bar I say, 'this is good' but I don't think you mean that kind of good.

THE MAN FROM THE LIGHTLESSNESS IN THE BACKSEAT: [*pauses, turns*] Yeah I think he's definitely good. Not candy-bar good. But good.

The driver rubs fog off the windshield with his sleeve.

THE DRIVER: I wish the whole world was candy-bar good, you know?

THE MAN FROM THE LIGHTLESSNESS IN THE BACKSEAT: I wish it was the other kind of good we just talked about.

THE DRIVER: Not candy-bar good?

The man from the lightlessness shakes his head, and opens the driver's door. Together they carry the body to the portable toilet.

THE DRIVER: [*taking a rock off the ground*] I will fill his mouth with this rock.

THE MAN FROM THE LIGHTLESSNESS IN THE BACKSEAT: [*nods*] Yes. He will not be allowed to float.

THE DRIVER: He will not be allowed to float [*puts stone in*] we will make him too heavy. He will be too heavy.

THE MAN FROM THE LIGHTLESSNESS IN THE BACKSEAT: It is good to make him too heavy. We are doing the thing that is right [*nods*] To keep the earth away from the ceiling of space, we do the thing that is right.

THE DRIVER: I agree. I hope his face becomes infected and gruesome and turns into something no one wants to see. The shit and bad water will get into his ripped face. When I am alone at my apartment and I hate the smell, I eat an orange and I squeeze the peels so they spray good smelling mist into the air. It helps I think. It helps somehow. I don't know what I'm talking about. It's just when I thought about the portable toilet I immediately thought of my apartment. But seriously,

I have no clue what I'm talking about.

THE MAN FROM THE LIGHTLESSNESS IN THE BACKSEAT: Yes, that sounds nice.

They throw the body into the portable toilet. It swings by the waist, face in the shit water. They stuff the head into the shit and garbage and submerge the entire body. Then they back away from the portable toilet to avoid the splash. The plastic door has ice on it. They stare at the ice as it receives pulsing red from the powerlines.

THE DRIVER: [*pointing at ice*] I like the way that looks.

THE MAN FROM THE LIGHTLESSNESS IN THE BACKSEAT: Me too.

THE DRIVER: Maybe the world isn't so bad.

They walk back to the car.

THE DRIVER: Hey do you have any gum? My mouth is dry. Way too dry [*pointing, with mock accusation*] Don't be a liar like you know who. Do you have any gum?

THE MAN FROM THE LIGHTLESSNESS IN THE BACKSEAT: No. I don't have any gum. But I can put some snow in your mouth if you want me to. I would do that for you. You know I would do that for you.

THE DRIVER: No thanks [*stops by the car and stands on the shoulder of the road*] Everything seems quiet now. Nothing is moving. I refuse to let anything upset me [*leans back on car, folding arms*] There is nothing that can upset me. It hasn't happened in a long time. I don't think it will ever happen again. Is that good or bad? Is that candy-bar good? We are in a secret armpit of the world and I am glad to be here with you. I really mean that.

THE MAN FROM THE LIGHTLESSNESS IN THE BACKSEAT: [*looking into forest, dizzy*] I am glad to be here with you too [*not blinking*] When I'm driving or walking late at night and I pass a building that has a light on inside and I can see someone inside, walking around—I feel great. I like to look at people who I know are not looking at me. That is something I don't think, that is something I know. I don't have any beliefs because I know everything. And I don't want to hear any more of your beliefs. They don't matter to me.

THE DRIVER: [*opening passenger-side door*] You want to sit up front with me?

THE MAN FROM THE LIGHTLESSNESS IN THE BACKSEAT: [*looks at mess*] No, thank you.

They hug. They drive away. The driver suggests they institute a change cup so as to easily purchase gum by collecting extra pennies and quarters. His suggestion is met with silence. They both think of things to say but say none of them. Driving. They return to the main road, and stop at red lights automatically, staring blinkless.

BE NICE TO EVERYONE [VERSION 2]

A man and a woman are taking a shower together in a small cold bathroom. The man watches as the water drains and the woman dips her head backwards under the showerhead, squeezes water out.

WOMAN: Are you done?

MAN: Yes. I'm done. Even though I know I will have to do this again, I'm done right now [*holds elbows in hands, shivering*] I'm done for now. Thank you.

The woman turns, talks to him over her shoulder.

WOMAN: You have been quiet.

MAN: [*watching the water*] I have been thinking about whether or not I could force your entire body down the drain.

WOMAN: [*blinking some water out of her eyes*] Thinking is a good way to keep from passing out and dying. Thinking is good for keeping yourself awake. Thinking is dirty air making its way into your head and collecting in a pile that you try to separate by grain-size [*spits water out*] Thinking is what makes your blood steam out through your pores and rise in a cloud that covers a piece of ground that no one is looking at.

MAN: [*crossing arms, the water hits his face*] Thank you for teaching me how to think.

The woman shuts the water off and steps out of the shower. She begins to towel off. The man stays in the shower, watching the water drain.

WOMAN: [*toweling her hair*] Why are you still standing there?

MAN: Do you ever worry that something is leaving with the water? And that it will never come back?

WOMAN: Not at all [*bends at waist and continues toweling her hair*] I want the water to leave. It has both of us in it. If it doesn't leave, we will continue to be together.

The man collects some of the water in his hands and drinks it. He gets out and takes the towel from her and dries off, preoccupied.

MAN: [*to himself*] I still think something is bothering me—maybe it isn't the water.

The man and the woman put their underwear on and face the mirror. They look at each other in the mirror, not themselves.

MAN: [*reaching past her to grab some deodorant*] I love you more than anything. Now that the water is in my stomach, nothing will change. We will continue to be together. You can hate me, but I will hold it in me forever. Even if it turns to boil and poisons me. Maybe the water will become my blood. I don't know. Whatever it is, I will hold it in.

WOMAN: [*combing hair, making eye contact in mirror*] Then I will cut it out of you [*pinching nose clean of water, wincing*] Can you hand me that lipstick behind you, on the windowsill?

MAN: [*turning*] Here you go.

WOMAN: [*reaching behind her*] Thanks, I bet— [*she stops, looks at her hand, then holds up a switchblade*] Nice try. You think this would kill me? You will never kill me. You will never be alone [*runs the switchblade over her mouth and gums*] You will never say goodbye to me [*rubs her lips together*] You will never be alone.

She kisses him on the mouth. Then looks him in the eyes, still holding his face.

WOMAN: You will never be alone.

MAN: That is one of my worries.

WOMAN: [*looking back at the mirror and putting deodorant on*] Why do you have worries? I never have worries. I don't. At all, ever. I don't. What are you worried about right now?

MAN: Right now [*putting toilet lid down and sitting on it*] I am worried that I am a man exactly my age, exactly the same as myself, and that I am right here. The worry is that I am that person right now. Basically.

WOMAN: [*putting deodorant on, shaking breasts, mocking*] You will never be that alone.

MAN: [*looking at his feet*] Stop saying that. It can't be true.

They continue what they're doing. Everything is quiet for a few minutes. They leave the bathroom and enter the woman's bedroom. The man turns on the ceilingfan light. On the wall it says, "I like you."

WOMAN: What the fuck.

MAN: Yeah. I wrote "I like you" on the lightbulb. I had to use two markers. At first I was using one marker but it like, died halfway through. And I wanted the letters to be legible. I thought about doing x's and o's but I didn't for some reason [*seems to think for a second, then focuses again*] I'm pretty satisfied with the results. I mean I didn't really have anything else to do this afternoon. Plus I was worried about just saying it to you. "I like you" is a stupid thing to say to someone. That was another one of my worries. But I figured you knew. Please don't hold it against me.

The blinds hit against the window and the woman is nervous, looking at random objects in the room.

WOMAN: The features of something are what make it unappealing.

The man and the woman watch the blinds hit against the window. She looks at the words, "I like you" on the wall and covers her mouth with her hand. Then she stands on the bed and licks the words off the lightbulb, pausing to let her burnt tongue recover from the painful searing.

WOMAN: [*straining*] Now I have made everything fine. There are sores on my tongue now. And I have made everything fine. If we both forget what happened, we won't let it impact our actions anymore. I have always wanted to say that I have made everything fine.

The woman bites into her swollen tongue to itch the welts. Her tongue pops and leaks down her chin. The burst tongue runs down her chin and chest. She gags on some of it. She gets off the bed and looks out the window.

WOMAN: [*looking through the waving blinds at the forest preserve in the distance*] I used to ride my bike back there [*craning her neck*] Until I got molested by a man in a raincoat [*laughing*] I heard the police shot him last week because they thought he was reaching into his pants for a gun. I have no feelings about that. I mean it feels good that the man in the raincoat is dead. That makes me feel good. Like, I think about it and envision the dead body with the bleeding hole, and that feels good. But maybe that's wrong. Maybe I should feel upset about the bleeding hole in his body. Everybody gets molested though. So it's cool. I don't hate him. Can you blame him? I'm good-looking.

MAN: I agree [*he approaches her, puts hands on her shoulders*] In many ways, I identify with this man in the raincoat. The man in the raincoat seems wonderful. He has good taste.

They laugh and high-five, turn back to the window. The man looks out the window at the dark patch of trees, his chin on her shoulder.

MAN: Maybe the man with the raincoat on was a great guy and just wanted to have sex with someone who didn't want it back or couldn't understand it. What did the man in the raincoat say while he was molesting you? Did he say anything? Or what?

WOMAN: Yes, he did.

MAN: What did he say?

WOMAN: He said, 'I am wearing this raincoat because I am afraid of rain.' [*pause*] Huh. He wasn't that mean to me actually.

The woman's cat runs up behind the man and bites his toes.

MAN: Fuck.

THE CAT: [*looking up*] Reer.

MAN: [*looking down*] You are the only living thing I like. You mean more to me than anything else. I can't explain that to you [*then slowly*] unless you understand me right now.

THE CAT: Reer.

MAN: Yes and my heart is big enough to cover you and put you to sleep.

THE CAT: [*looking to the side*] Reer.

MAN: Don't argue with me, we are in love and this is how it will be.

THE CAT: Reer [*bites the man's toe again then runs away*]

MAN: [*looks back at the woman*] Our relationship—that is, mine and the cat's—it needs some work. But I'm willing to try. I think we can resolve our differences [*walks to the closet*] wait, I forgot [*reaching into backpack, hands the woman a present*] Here you go. When I saw these I totally thought of you. I had to get them for you.

WOMAN: [*opening present*] I'm excited. Thank you for parting my absolute self-hatred with a meaningless object.

MAN: [*laughs a little*] I dare you to come back to life.

The woman continues to unwrap the paper. When she's finished removing the paper, she opens the box, looks in. There is nothing inside. She sits on the bed and laughs. The man puts his shoes on to leave.

WOMAN: [*staring out the window*] I am impressed that you wake up and act like nothing is wrong with who you are. That you put on clothes and feed your body to keep it alive. In order to do what?

MAN: [*balancing on one leg, putting on his shoe*] I'm keeping myself alive to see the day you beg me to bleed in your mouth so you can stay alive. I am waiting. I set up expectations so I have something to look forward to. There is only waiting. And I will get what I want. And my hands will make it black. Everything is mine and you are going to beg me.

Sound of footsteps in the apartment above. Then quiet. The woman watches the man tie his shoes.

WOMAN: You are the master of treating people around you like they are worthless. And I want to learn everything you know. So please—be honest with me and tell me everything you know about treating people like they are worthless. I said please. Take note of that [*wipes chin with bedsheet*] Be my teacher. Be honest.

A car passes outside the window. Then another. Gone. A man wearing a raincoat stands from below the window and stares at the people in the apartment.

MAN: If we are being honest, sometimes I imagine that I am in a miniature fighter plane and I'm flying around your head dropping bombs on your face. I imagine it because I think actually doing it would be impossible. Or cost too much.

WOMAN: Is that why sometimes I wake up to you dropping little rolled up pieces of tinfoil on my face while making explosion sounds?

MAN: Yes. It is. I'm surprised it has taken this long for you to ask me about that. I am in love with a war that never ends, involving things that never die. And I love you more than anything. I hope the lightbulb explained it all.

They sit there thinking about when and how to make up an excuse to leave. They think about excuses then test them for potential weaknesses. They each know that every excuse to leave will be weak in some way.

WOMAN: You are quiet again.

MAN: If you turn around for a second, I'll give you a surprise. Do you promise not to look?

WOMAN *turns around.*

MAN: No. You have to say that you promise.

WOMAN: I promise not to turn around [*long pause*] I promise. Ok?

There is no response. She turns back around and sees the man lying on the ground, facedown.

WOMAN: Hey—hey are you ok?

He doesn't move.

WOMAN: [*louder*] Are you ok?

Silence. The man slowly turns over.

MAN: [*lifting his head*] Yes. I'm fine. I just wanted to make you think something happened to me. I think that was enough. I think that's enough yeah. I'm satisfied [*sits on the bed with her*] Everything is great.

The woman looks at the floor, wiping her chin with the blanket.

MAN: You are quiet now.

WOMAN: I am hoping our weight will make the bed fall into the earth.

MAN: I know what you mean.

A breeze pulls the blinds towards the outside. The man in the raincoat is still watching them.

CANCER KILLS [2]

The livingroom of an empty apartment, lights off. A man wearing a bathrobe sits on the tilefloor. His phone vibrates next to him and he picks it up. Stares at it.

MAN IN BATHROBE: Hello?

OTHER PERSON: Hey.

MAN IN BATHROBE: [*looks around, can't see anything*] Who is this?

OTHER PERSON: Hey, you want to go to a concert tonight? I'm meeting up with a bunch of people downtown and they're celebrating somebody's birthday—or, I don't know—and we're going to a bar, then this concert. You want to go?

The man in the bathrobe looks at the dead bugs on his floor and the crumbs covering the bottoms of his feet. He puts the phone to his other ear and flicks some of the crumbs off his feet. He doesn't respond. He notices a cricket moving across the floor in awkward, sideways flips.

OTHER PERSON: So did you want—

MAN IN BATHROBE: There's a cricket on my floor [*leaning forward*] I think its leg is broken maybe.

OTHER PERSON: What are you talking about?

MAN IN BATHROBE: [*flicks more crumbs, aiming at cricket*] It keeps trying to move but it can't.

OTHER PERSON: [*pause*] I don't care.

MAN IN BATHROBE: It can't move.

He looks out the window in his kitchen. The trees outside are thin. They shake violently. But are quiet.

MAN IN BATHROBE: I'm thinking about killing it [*long pause*] the cricket. Or maybe I should just let it go beneath the cabinet [*crosses legs beneath him*] Then it'll have to starve to die, but that can be done alone. Then again, I could kill it [*seems to be talking to himself now*] I definitely could kill it. Easily. There was another cricket in my bathtub, last night I think. Are you listening? [*pause*] There are a lot of crickets in my apartment. I want you to hear about the cricket in the bathtub [*switches hands and scratches sore ear*] ok, so I went to brush my teeth last night and there was a cricket, on the lower curve of the tub. It just sat there, looking straight up, like, "fuck, what now?" I know bugs probably don't have any emotions, but, maybe. It's whole body looked like an emotion. Does that make sense? [*to himself*] Not sure. Are you listening? I could see words or feelings just by looking at it. I watched it for a while and then washed it down the drain. And that was that.

The man in the bathrobe flicks crumbs off his feet and watches the shaking trees. A small twig hits his window. Then there is quiet.

OTHER PERSON: Do you want to come out with us then?

MAN IN BATHROBE: Ok [*clears throat*] I'll go. Even though I don't know who you are. Even though I hate you. I'll go [*stands*] But I'm just going out to kill time. If I spend one more minute alone, I might put my head through the kitchen window in an attempt to become sleep. Would that even work? [*seems to remember phone*] Alright? Alright so, I'll go. But I hate you and—I hate you.

OTHER PERSON: When should we pick you up? Are you ready now?

The man in the bathrobe looks at the floor again for the cricket, but can't find it. He rubs crumbs off his foot again, balancing on one leg.

MAN IN BATHROBE: Give me like ten minutes to get dressed—

The other end hangs up. Sound of dead line.

MAN IN BATHROBE: [*still holding phone to his ear*] Actually I can't remember if I own any clothing now or not. Seems hard to remember [*confused*] Maybe I could cover my body with the crumbs and the bugs. They will cover me when I sleep anyway. They can be my clothing. They will always be there.

He throws the phone against the wall and walks through the kitchen, out the front door. Outside, he stands on his doorstep and stares over the wooden fence at the trees. There is a garbagebag stuck in one of the trees. He stares at the garbagebag.

MAN IN BATHROBE: [*points at garbagebag*] The garbagebag will always be there [*pause, hand back at side*] The garbagebag will always be there.

Sound of people walking down the sidewalk. The man in the bathrobe kneels below his wooden fence. Through a slat in the wooden fence, he watches the sidewalk. There's a group of girls hugging each other out front of an apartment across from his. They all carry gifts. The girl at the door lets them into the orange light of her apartment.

MAN IN BATHROBE: Her and her orange light will always be there.

Still kneeling, he watches them through the fence and the window, into the orange light. Their voices mute, he can see them smiling and laughing and making gestures with their hands. He watches them talk, holding his bathrobe closed. At one point he ducks down as if someone has seen him.

MAN IN BATHROBE: I wish I had shoes, or knew where my shoes were. Are the people here to pick me up? [*pause*] The people will always be there to pick me up.

He returns to watching the girls, holding his bathrobe closed.

MAN IN BATHROBE: I wonder if I'll ever be a grandfather.

THE HUMAN BODY AS A FIREPLACE

A single story house. Halloween party. Crowds of people in or around the house. In one of the rooms, by herself, there is a girl dressed like the sun, sitting on her bed looking at a stuffed whale on the floor.

GIRL SUN: I'm going to kill myself [*nudges stuffed whale with toe*] Hey, you, stupid fucking stuffed whale—I'm going to kill you, then myself. That's how it will be, you know? First you, then me, and then us both. Done. Hey, stupid fucking stuffed whale guy. Do you want to see it? Huh? I bet you want to see it. You want to see it happen [*stepping on stuffed whale*] I used to feel gross after you would come in me. Now I feel like it doesn't matter. I just feel a little uncomfortable, like when your leg touches the shower curtain and feels the cold from older drops. Fuck you. You ruined me. Hey, whale man—

Sound of people talking outside her bedroom window, bush branches hitting the frame. The girl dressed like the sun gets off her bed and looks out the window. From below, near a bush, a person dressed like a happy face is taking the time to assist another person dressed like a frowning face. They kneel down and lie next to each other underneath the bush.

FROWNING FACE: It's so dark under here. Will there be flowers here then?

HAPPY FACE: No, there will not. There will be nothing here [*puts arms around the person dressed like a frowning face and spoons her*] Just me and you. With our magnet eyelashes.

Then from above there is intense light. They squint and look up. And in the window stands the girl dressed like the sun.

HAPPY FACE: [*looking up through branches of bush*] The sun always promises more. It is never pretty.

FROWNING FACE: [*covers eyes with hand*] Yeah, go away.

In the window, the girl dressed like the sun is quiet. She shakes her head, tearing up. Then she leaves her room, enters the crowded main area of the house. The house is filled with people. There's a person dressed like Frederick Douglas, someone dressed like an Oreo, a large group of people dressed like priests, someone dressed like a KKK member with an afro, a giant worm on the ground writhing, comprising multiple people, and others dressed like nothing. Many others. The girl dressed like the sun gets mixed in, passing the priests spread quietly across the main area. And in walks a girl wearing a pet store employee shirt.

PRIEST: [*reaching out*] Hey, you work at the pet store for real?

PET STORE GIRL: Yeah.

PRIEST: Alright good—got a little question for you then [*puts thin cigar out on wall*] Can you feed a goldfish cookies? Or, uh, juice? To keep it alive I mean.

PET STORE GIRL: [*touching her hair*] I don't think so.

OTHER PRIEST: [*sitting inside open windowsill facing out the house, touching the paint with his fingers*] Fucking told you man.

There is general yelling from all the people. A man wearing only a condom steps forward.

MAN WEARING CONDOM: Try taffy. Goldfish love taffy I think.

PET STORE GIRL: Yeah, maybe. Ok—bye.

She falls to the carpet, her head withering to nothing then reforming, and repeating. A group watches her head vanish and return. And the priests pray, kneeling over the degenerating head. The man wearing only a condom walks away from the larger group and goes to the bathroom. He takes off the condom and starts pissing in the toilet. In the bathtub there is a guy sleeping. The guy is naked, and covered in grass clippings and wet leaves. All stuck to him.

GUY IN BATHTUB: [*mumbling, still asleep*] Thanksgiving is for pussies [*starts moaning*] no way—no way. Stop. Uh, no way.

He wakes up and looks at the man pissing. And focuses slowly. Outside the bathroom people are yelling and laughing and some are not saying anything or making any sound.

MAN PISSING: Hey sleepy-head.

GUY IN BATHTUB: [*breathily*] Hey. How're you today? [*grassclippings and leaves fall off him*]

MAN PISSING: [*flushes, puts condom back on*] Good [*nodding*] I'm doing good today.

GUY IN BATHTUB: Good [*he turns over onto his other shoulder, toppling more grass and leaves*] Oh, hey, there's an antibacterial hand rinse by the sink—I think you should try it. Says it'll kill 99.9% of the germs on your hands [*he yawns loudly, coughs*] There are probably a lot of germs on your hands. The germs are everywhere. You should kill all of them. Make them pay.

MAN WEARING CONDOM: [*making last adjustment to condom, then stretching his arms*] Hell yeah—kill them all—those assholes.

GUY IN BATHUB: [*quietly, his back turned*] Yes, all of them. When all the germs are dead we can stop worrying. We can start making new germs.

MAN WEARING CONDOM: Thank you. Thank you for wanting that. Do you want me to kill the germs on you?

GUY IN BATHTUB: [*returning to sleep*] No thanks.

MAN WEARING CONDOM: Ok.

The man wearing a condom washes his hands and then walks out. There are more people in the kitchen and connected livingroom, and some are drawing on the walls with thin markers. He rejoins the larger group of people and grabs an open beer off the kitchen table. And the man wearing the condom looks inside his beer can with one eye closed. With a person dressed like Superman watching from behind.

SUPERMAN: [*to man wearing condom*] What are you doing?

MAN WEARING CONDOM: I'm making sure no spiders got inside. [*opens closed eye and takes sip*] I'm totally afraid of that. I don't want a spider to bite my mouth and then die on my tongue. 1. Because it would probably hurt and 2. Because that would be a scary death for the spider. You know?

Before Superman answers, someone wearing a janitor one-piece walks into the kitchen. The janitor lowers the one-piece to his waist and grabs a big knife from the pumpkin on the counter. And grabs Superman.

THE JANITOR: Hey faggot. Hey, faggot [*presses himself into the man dressed like Superman*] Look at me. You faggot. Look [*presses crotch onto superman's leg*] If I cut myself, will you fucking drink it faggot? Will you drink it off me faggot? Would you do that? You fucking faggot. Faggot motherfucker.

Superman covers his mouth with both hands. Shakes his head.

THE JANITOR: Don't be worried about your mouth. Worry that I am too clean to drink.

Superman takes his hands off his mouth.

SUPERMAN: [*toneless, unblinking*] Do it then.

The janitor jabs at his own stomach area with the knife a few times. Nothing happens. Nothing happens and he tries harder and then there is a popping sound. Blood. A hole leaks blood down the janitor's stomach.

THE JANITOR: Do you want to be saved faggot? By my blood? You faggot. Do you want to drink my blood you faggot and be saved from being a faggot?

People circle, say nothing. They watch. And Superman kneels. He puts his head under the janitor's stomach, licking off some of the blood. When trying a big mouthful right from the hole though, he can't swallow, very salty and thick. And he gags. The crowd claps.

PRIEST 1: How do you feel?

PRIEST 2: Yeah how does it feel faggot?

PRIEST 3: You're saved now.

PRIEST 4: You faggot.

PRIEST 1: How do you feel?

SUPERMAN: [*stain-faced, lying on floor, sickened in the janitor's shadow*] I feel like nothing is different.

The janitor leaves. Circle disperses. Someone dressed like Santa Claus approaches Superman.

SANTA CLAUS: [*looking down*] You know, you need to find a way to kill him. He is going to kill you man. You need to find a way to kill him first. I can't help you, but I trust you to figure out how to kill him on your own. Do you understand me? Also, do you know who lives here? Because I kind of fucked up the toilet. Just so you know. There's water all over the floor. [*makes like he is going to say something else, then leaves*]

Superman spits out some blood on the floor and looks at the kitchen ceiling. The walls and ceiling of the kitchen are covered in drawings done in marker. And they lead along the walls and ceiling into the livingroom. On the couch in the livingroom, three people sit watching a cooking show. One of the three is asleep, and one wears sunglasses with neon yellow arms and another man is not dressed like anything identifiable. The television is atop a partially smashed cardboard box.

MAN WITHOUT COSTUME: [*to the man with neon glasses*] What are you supposed to be?

EXTRA FROM SURFING MOVIE: [*lifts neon sunglasses*] I'm an extra from a surfing movie. What are you?

MAN WITHOUT COSTUME: I'm a bruise.

The extra from a surfing movie nods and looks around a little, quickly confused for some reason then composed.

EXTRA FROM SURFING MOVIE: Fair enough man. Fair enough. Aw, Goddamn it [*gesturing to the tv*] That's way too much fucking cilantro man [*kicks the sleeping guy*] Right man? Right?

The sleeping guy turns a little and opens his eyes. His eyes part sore to the light.

SLEEPING MAN: What? [*clears throat*] Huh? Fuck you, Craig. [*back to sleep, cradled by the couch arm*]

EXTRA FROM SURFING MOVIE: [*to man dressed as bruise*] We always fight in public. It kills me [*then points to tv*] No don't put the fucking lemon zest on yet. Fucking shit [*stomping his feet in alteration*] Bull. Ass. Shit.

THE BRUISE: [*nodding to the sleeping man*] What's he supposed to be? Like, what's he dressed as.

EXTRA FROM SURFING MOVIE: [*still staring at the cooking show*] He's a Vampire—A Tit Vampire. But he's gonna fucking starve if he sleeps through the night. [*kicks tit vampire again*]

TIT VAMPIRE: [*lips pinched open by the couch's arm*] Fah koo. [*puts his arms behind head*]

The Tit Vampire wears a white t-shirt with the words "Tit Vampire" written in marker on the front. And there's a single red line on either side of his mouth, drawn to look like blood.

EXTRA FROM SURFING MOVIE: [*kicks the Tit Vampire*] Hey, do the thing.

TIT VAMPIRE: Nah man. [*breathes out heavily and tries not to smile*] Nah man.

THE BRUISE: Do it.

The extra from surfing movie kicks the *Tit Vampire again. The Tit Vampire coughs, opens his eyes.*

TIT VAMPIRE: [*in mumbling, quietly-laughing Transylvanian accent*] I vant to sock your tit. Blah—I vant to sock your tit.

They all laugh.

TIT VAMPIRE: [*positioning himself for sleep again*] Fah koo man.

Two men walk past, through the livingroom. One of them is dressed like a 'Rhino Stripper' and the other dressed like Elvis. The Rhino Stripper stops, looks at the tv.

RHINO STRIPPER: That's too much cilantro man.

They exit the house out a sliding glass door at the back of the livingroom. Outside it's raining a little, and almost morning. They go behind the garage, to the alley. They piss together in the alley. Elvis zips first, and picks up his cigarette from a nearby cinderblock. He looks up and down the dark alley while the Rhino Stripper continues pissing. A skinny raccoon comes out from the side of the garage and bites him on the leg. Hissing, rabid.

RHINO STRIPPER: Motherfucker [*gets raccoon facedown by the neck, and lifts it eyelevel*] You FUCK.

It hisses and scratches his face. Rabid. He grabs its whiskers and pulls them until they come from out of the face. The raccoon screams, clawing. And the Rhino Stripper drops the raccoon, kicks it into the plywood wall of the garage. He kicks it deep, creating a hole. Broken arms and legs swing out through the hole. And blood follows—through the clumped hair and the splintered wall, in a long dilation. Elvis and the Rhino Stripper watch the dilation.

ELVIS: That thing is dead [*pause*] I am looking at a dead thing. The hole is holding a dead thing [*points*] Look at the reverse birth.

RHINO STRIPPER: [*points a forefinger at the bleeding hole and clicks his thumb*] Happy Birthday [*looks around*] Guess what, I feel a whole lot better. I really do. I feel like those women in yogurt commercials must feel, like I'm free and airy, you know? I feel like a woman. [*kneels by the raccoon*] Here, help me.

The raccoon is stuck in the wall as the men try to remove it. They tug it out. When it comes free its face is an uninhabited sock puppet. Elvis holds it, examining. He puts it on his head, blood dripping down behind his jeweled sunglasses, and into his fake cottony black sideburns.

ELVIS: You need a hat? Maybe a little purse or something?

RHINO STRIPPER: No thank you.

ELVIS: Ok then.

Elvis throws the raccoon corpse up into a tree across the alley. And the two men stand staring at where it went but can't really see it. Still too dark for far-sight.

ELVIS: [*looking in direction of raccoon*] I remember before I lived here, I lived in Brookfield.

RHINO STRIPPER: [*yawning*] Where?

ELVIS: Brookfield. It's like a half hour away from here. That was the only other town I lived in. There were always raccoons tearing up the lawn and the fucking garbage and shit. All the time [*picks up rock from alley and throws it in direction of raccoon stuck in tree*] My dad set a trap one night [*rock clinks against fence*] And two days later there was a huge raccoon, biting at the rungs of the trap. My dad asked me to help him carry it down behind our tool shed [*throws another rock*] Out of view from the neighbors [*clink*] He set the cage down and brought out a small caliber gun. He started shooting the raccoon. It was point blank right at face and neck and stomach. After like four shots [*pause, throw, clink*] it was screaming and thrashing. Fucking bleeding all over the ground and the cage. Real big watery drops [*wipes rain off mouth*] And my dad got this really weak look on his face. He kept asking me to look away whenever he shot. He even put his face into the crook of his elbow at one point, as he shot. It took like twenty shots to fucking kill the raccoon. Thing was pissed [*throws rock at garage*] But it fought with some meaning man—I don't even know. It fought for its shitty little life like its shitty little life meant something [*lightly jabs the Rhino Stripper's arm*] Hey, do I sound like Elvis at all?

The Rhino Stripper stares.

RHINO STRIPPER: Were you trying to?

ELVIS: [*looks away, throws another rock*] Not really.

They continue to throw rocks up the tree, hitting nothing but the eventual ground. Clinking. More people now around the backyard, some entering the garage.

ELVIS: Hey—do you think raccoons get halos too?

RHINO STRIPPER: That raccoon would need a really bent up halo [*throwing rock*] Should we fill the bloody hole we've made with rocks, to grow more raccoons?

ELVIS: No.

The Rhino Stripper throws a rock at a parked car, wiping his muddy hands off on his g-string and then his plastic rhino nose. A broken bottle sounds from inside the garage behind them. People yelling.

RHINO STRIPPER: [*acknowledges garage sounds and then looks up vaguely at the air*] If it keeps misting like this we'll be able to see a rainbow in an hour probably [*turns to Elvis*] You know?

A pause.

ELVIS: So what?

RHINO STRIPPER: [*throws rock, clinking sound*] Good point.

They stand next to each other, staring out at the woods. Sound of light rain and people in the garage. Then a loud bump from the other side of the garage wall behind them. And more yelling. Inside the garage everyone is standing, and screaming something that can't be discerned over the other screaming. Off to the side there's a couch and some garbage cans. And the janitor has another man—dressed like a ballerina—against the garage wall, arm around the ballerina's neck. The strain of squeezing the ballerina's throat fills the janitor's neck-veins into definition. Long scratch marks cover the janitor's face, where the ballerina has scratched, and is still scratching. People yell at what is happening and yell more when the ballerina pulls his head out, stepping back. The ballerina breathes long breaths then, face looking raw and pulled, one ear ripped along the top arch bleeding. Someone throws a bottle at him but it misses and hits the ceiling, doesn't even break. After a few breaths the ballerina comes at the janitor and swings. The janitor avoids it by moving his head to the side, and the ballerina hits his barehand hard against the wall. He recoils, and holds the already smeared knuckles. He steps back, unable to yell.

SOMEONE IN THE CROWD: [*turns to someone else*] Why are they fighting?

A bottle hits the wall by the janitor and rains on the ground.

SOMEONE ELSE: The janitor guy wanted the guy in the ballerina costume to admit he likes the show "Cheers" [*shaking head*] He wouldn't admit it. They agreed to let whoever wins neuter the loser.

I personally, I fucking love Cheers.

SOMEONE ELSE: Me too.

SOMEONE ELSE: [*pushing forward to see*] Yeah it's not that bad.

The janitor punches the ballerina in the face. Repeatedly. Thick slapping sounds follow each punch. And the ballerina falls, but keeps getting up. More punches. Bleeding from his eyes and nose, he keeps getting up. One of the punches though, he falls, and his broken hand goes beneath him, bending. He has trouble getting up. And a priest steps from the crowd and kills the ballerina with a brick to the back of the head. Then the crowd swarms the ballerina. They kick him. Ribs cave. Face caves. Everything in the kicking gets caved. And the priests take out box cutters and cut long lines into the back and stomach area while others continue to kick. One of the priests pulls down the ballerina's shoulder straps and the other priests cut. Then a priest in a holier robe comes up and hands the janitor a pair of long scissors. The janitor leans over the body while lower priests violently remove the ballerina's underwear. And the janitor cuts off the ballerina's genitals, one hand on each scissor handle.

THE JANITOR: [*to the priests*] One of you light the couch on fire so we can send him to Heaven when I am done.

One of the priests empties a gas canister onto the couch. From the silence, a dry burst. The couch fiber curls. And smoke fills the garage, gradual.

SOMEONE IN THE CROWD: [*smoke thinly around his head and face*] I thought neutering was when you cut someone's lips off.

The janitor stares at the blood pooling between the ballerina's legs. He puts his hand over his mouth, disappointed.

THE JANITOR: Oh man [*takes hand from mouth, purses lips*] Shit. I didn't know that [*cuts the lips off the ballerina's face in two struggling snips*] There we go.

SOMEONE ELSE IN THE CROWD: [*coughing*] You guys, I hate to say it, but I think neutering is when you cut off someone's ears.

SOMEONE ELSE: Yeah, I thought so too. I was going to say something.

The janitor frowns, rubs his chin. He cuts off the ears and everything else on the ballerina's face. There's much more smoke in the garage.

THE JANITOR: Ok [*hands up, fingers splayed, still holding scissors*] Is everyone happy?

The crowd is quiet. Couch fire has a sound though.

SOMEONE ELSE IN THE CROWD: Yeah, I'm good.

SOMEONE ELSE: Me too. I'm good.

One of the priests steps forward.

PRIEST: [*nervous*] But, God won't let him into Heaven without a recognizable face.

No one answers. Everyone leaves, the couch burning hard. The janitor opens the garage door and a wet breeze balances the heat, ushering out a canopy of smoke along the ceiling. The last of the people leave with the smoke. When the smoke's gone, only the janitor and one of the priests remain. She and the janitor move the couch out of the garage, each on one leg using the other leg to give a quick push . They hold hands to stay balanced and eventually it is out in the backyard. They stare at the flames. Quiet in the backyard.

THE JANITOR: Want to go for a walk? I don't think I'm going to be able to sleep right now.

PRIEST: Sure.

The janitor offers the priest a hand.

PRIEST: [*putting hands in pockets*] No thanks.

THE JANITOR: [*looking at crumpled body on the flaming couch*] There is still a thing called the world.

PRIEST: [*looking out vaguely towards the front yard*] There is still no way to tell where you are at on the curve.

THE JANITOR: There is still no way to think about there not being a world [*staring at the flaming couch*] Let's go. I want to eventually be able to sleep. The thing called the world will put out the fire on the couch.

They walk out of the backyard and down the driveway. The night is warm and light purple and almost done.

THE JANITOR: Something about right now makes me want to jump straight into the air and float away without saying goodbye to anyone.

The priest says nothing. And they pass two girls standing beneath the trim of the house, sharing a bottle. The two girls standing beneath the trim walk the opposite way, towards the flaming couch. One is dressed as her own grandmother and the other as a police officer. They walk up to the mangled corpse and watch it burn.

GRANDMOTHER: Is that a boy doggy or a girl doggy?

POLICE OFFICER: [*puts face closer*] I don't know, but I know it's not a doggy.

They watch the body burn and turn black with the couch. And the grandmother takes a wrist out of the fire then puts the broken fingers up to her chin.

GRANDMOTHER: [*trying to keep the bloody bones away from her mouth*] Hmmm. Am I a boy or girl? Or am I doggy? Who knows [*shaking broken fingers*] Hmmmm.

She gets some blood in her mouth, spits. They laugh.

POLICE OFFICER: [*laughing*] Jesus H.

GRANDMOTHER: [*shaking the broken fingers at the police officer*] Hey! Be a good girl, or satan will rape you in hell [*swallows, then begins to cough violently*] Fuck. Oh fuck. It's in my mouth.

The grandmother hunches over, coughing and gagging. She shakes and the police officer holds her until eventually she vomits out half of a very large jawbone. It hits the ground by their feet. And the grandmother wipes off the bile that hangs from her teeth, using her forearm.

POLICE OFFICER: [*still holding her*] Are you done?

The grandmother touches her throat and hacks some more.

GRANDMOTHER: Yeah. I'm good [*spits*] Thanks.

POLICE OFFICER: [*nervous, looking at jawbone on the grass*] You feel better right?

GRANDMOTHER: [*still touching throat*] Yeah. I feel great. Uh huh. [*spits*] Better.

The police officer kicks the jawbone beneath a bush. Looks in its direction.

POLICE OFFICER: [*nodding*] I thought you looked sick tonight. I'm glad you feel better though. I was worried all night.

GRANDMOTHER: [*coughing a little, raspy*] You were right [*makes face and begins to scratch underneath skirt*] You were definitely right. Fuck [*still scratching underneath skirt*] My legs itch. I need to shave [*looks at her friend*] Can you shave me? Can you shave my legs? I always cut myself bad. And then I feel weak and alone. The cuts are sometimes hard to keep clean. Can you do it? I know you will shave me good. I believe in you.

POLICE OFFICER: Get a razor. Do you have a razor? I'll do it if you get a razor and I don't have to move.

GRANDMOTHER: No wait [*walks off*] Here.

The grandmother takes the police officer by the hand, to the bush. They reach into the bush searching, and the grandmother retrieves the jawbone. She throws it against the driveway and the teeth break away, making the inside curve sharp. She throws it against the ground more, then picks it up. Soon she holds it against the mild sky light, bone now thinned and curved acutely. The grandmother puts her hand on the hose faucet. She turns on the hose and lets it run by their feet while they mud her legs completely with cupped handfuls. Grass floats in the pooling. Grass covers their bare feet. The rain lightens to being gone. And the grandmother puts her hand on the police officer's shoulder, balancing.

GRANDMOTHER: Good [*looks at her friend*] now, will you be a gentle boy? I'm just asking. Don't get offended. Will you be a gentle boy?

POLICE OFFICER: I'm not a boy silly. I'm a girl. And yes, I will. My mom taught me how to be gentle while hurting someone. Hand that to me and I promise I will be a good boy, I mean girl [*laughs*] I mean I will help you.

GRANDMOTHER: [*hands jawbone over*] Thank you for doing this [*wobbling*] I'm glad you're helping me.

POLICE OFFICER: Fine.

The police officer begins shaving in long motions up and down the grandmother's legs. Red blotches show beneath the mud. The grandmother clenches up. Pissing a little, she begins to moan. Then she pisses even harder. The police officer shaves her, upper thighs down to the tops of the feet. More cuts form. And the police officer uses the hose to douse the cuts.

POLICE OFFICER: [*looking up*] Your veins are not helping you now huh.

GRANDMOTHER: [*in strangely deep voice*] Then your mouth will you fucking pervert. Clean me off you fucking pervert bastard. Clean me even when you're done.

The police officer runs her hand up the leg and puts her fingers into the grandmother, grandmother again pissing hard.

GRANDMOTHER: [*head back, eyes closed, loud*] Clean me off you fucking pervert bastard.

The police officer puts her fingers all the way in. Then she takes her fingers out and puts them into the wet grass and mud. She lifts her muddy fingers and pushes them into the grandmother again. Neither looks at the other. The hose is still running. The grandmother still pissing, taking huge breaths and moaning.

GRANDMOTHER: [*looking down, eyes barely open, destroyed*] I fucking hate you. Clean off my cuts, you fucking pervert. You fucking pervert bastard. Clean them out [*screams*] Wipe them off.

The police officer doesn't respond. She takes a handful of mud and forces it into the grandmother. Then wipes her fingers on the grass. They stare at each other. Both kneel next to each other, and drink water from the pooling on the lawn.

GRANDMOTHER: [*stopping, turning*] We are doggies. Don't you think?

POLICE OFFICER: You're welcome [*wipes mouth, stands*]

The grandmother stands too, leaking mud down her legs. She smears it with her hand.

GRANDMOTHER: Thanks.

POLICE OFFICER: I know. I know.

They walk to the front yard. The grandmother sits on the front step, watching the street, with the police officer standing next to her, arms crossed. It's morning. And across the street, a young girl dressed like a princess sits on the curb, picking through a plastic pumpkin filled with candy. She waves from across the street and they wave back to her.

GRANDMOTHER: [*pointing to cuts on her leg*] What is this?

POLICE OFFICER: [*still waving to princess*] Those are cuts.

GRANDMOTHER: [*nods, points to the ground*] What is this?

POLICE OFFICER: That is the ground.

GRANDMOTHER: [*pointing at police officer*] What is this?

POLICE OFFICER: This is your friend.

The princess walks across the street to them and holds out a candybar. She pushes the melted candy bar out of the wrapper, bites it. They divide it three ways, one bite each, and they watch morning happen. The grandmother wipes the mud-trickle off with her hand again, then points at the princess.

GRANDMOTHER: [*to the police officer*] What's this?

POLICE OFFICER: I don't know.

FRIENDSHIP IS NICENESS AND IS

A restaurant. Six a.m. Satan and Khhkr sit at a table. They're tired-looking, him and her both. And just outside the window, a planter levels the wall. The planter is empty, except for dead roots and small gray leaves. And snow comes down lightly, and some hits their window.

SATAN: [*looks from empty planter to Khhkr*] The planter is empty. Nothing grows there now [*moves face closer across table, smiles*] What's your favorite kind of jelly? I want to know things about you so I can recount them and act like we have a bond, even though it is only time that makes us similar.

KHHKR: My favorite kind of jelly is the kind that has your ground-up heart in it [*makes kissy face—then concerned*] I keep thinking I am about to laugh, but it will not happen for some reason. There is probably a huge laugh in my body somewhere all lost and confused. I feel pity for it.

Satan looks out the window. He stares, touching some hair on his face. The snow continues down with the same infrequency.

SATAN: Breathe out onto this window and see if you can find the laugh, and if the laugh is there, take it out and laugh it. That's what I would do. And that's what you should do.

Khhkr looks around the restaurant, extending her neck.

KHHKR: Maybe someone here stole the laugh then. Someone has to have it. Should we look for it?

SATAN: [*still staring out window*] I don't want to get up let's just sit here [*long silence*] Stop talking to me.

KHHKR: Ok. Tell me if eventually you are wanting to get up and help me look for it though [*pause*] A fire's best friend is a big enough hole to hold it and make it look brighter and meaner. Do you get that? Do you see what I'm saying.

Satan nods. He drinks his water. Sees his empty glass and seems to panic but remains still. Remains still and slowly hides the glass behind the napkin holder to avoid alerting Khhkr. And puts his hands on the table. Amused.

SATAN: I would say that, apple jelly is my favorite. [*hits both hands on tabletop hard*] Apple.

Khhkr picks up her fork and touches the prongs to Satan's face. He remains as amused, both hands still on the table top.

KHHKR: Oh yeah? That's your favorite?

In the street directly outside, two construction workers are talking. The one laughs. The other continues to talk, placing a hand on the laughing man's shoulder. They are close to each other and they are saying things, things that the other can respond to and add to and eventually walk away from, done. Satan watches them.

SATAN: I'm not listening to you. I'm watching the construction workers talk. For some reason right now I envy them.

Khhkr takes the fork away from his face. Then she crosses her legs and dumps a sugar packet out onto the table.

KHHKR: You're so cute [*moving sugar grains with two fingers*] Every time you smile, I have to change my underwear.

She spreads the grains around and clicks her tongue a little. A child passes them, holding a plate.

CHILD: [*stopping*] The laughs are everywhere. You have to steal them. They don't come to you. [*he walks off*]

SATAN: Sorry about not wanting to help you get your laughs back. They will come somehow [*blowing the sugar onto her lap*] Just don't be mean. You smell so nice in the morning and your eyes are always just the right amount of puffy. Why be mean? Why ruin that?

The waitress comes. They both order.

WAITRESS: [*raises eyebrows*] Is that all?

Satan looks at his lap.

SATAN: That's all.

The waitress collects the menus.

WAITRESS: Ruin as many lives as you can and be an artist about it [*putting pen in front pocket*] I'll be right back.

She leaves. Through the window the sky is purple, and from the purple comes the snow—paced the same, slowly. They both watch, trying to trace flake paths but really just staring. And at one point they accidentally look at each other. When this happens Khhkr opts for staring at the table, and Satan stares out the window and sometimes at his lap.

SATAN: I think that each snowflake feels cheated no matter where it lands [*clears throat*] Or it should.

KHHKR: It should. And I love you. And we are snowflakes.

She touches Satan's hand across the table. He puts his other hand over hers.

SATAN: At night your breath is my blanket [*grabs glass*] It is the only thing I still enjoy [*takes small sip of melted ice*] Do you still want me to cut your hair today?

KHHKR: Yes [*pause*] Yes I do. I want that.

SATAN: Would you like that?

Khhkr nods. Their meals come and they eat in silence. Stare the meal to completion. Satan keeps looking at the dead plants in the planter.

SATAN: The construction workers are gone.

KHHKR: They are at home in their closets, hanging from electrical cords.

Silence again. Khhkr opens more sugar packets, distracted. Some people get up and leave from a table nearby. Another family walks past, towards the open table. The entire family stops, and looks quietly at Khhkr and Satan. The entire family shakes their heads no. Then they take the open table and converse quietly with each other.

KHHKR: [*flicking sugar, watching fingers*] When I was walking home yesterday I walked across a parking lot and there was a children's book in a puddle. It was this book where there's a frog who learns about friendship by becoming friends with a fly named Chad. I learned how to treat you by reading the book. I just sat in the puddle and read the book and learned how to be your friend. I want to burn animals. Ok? Ok, good.

She leans over and tries to kiss Satan. Satan moves. Then stares out the window.

SATAN: Don't touch me. I'm too happy to enjoy it [*craning neck*] Where did the construction workers go? You need to tell me.

KHHKR: I wasn't going to kiss you, I was going to bite your face off and suck out the laugh you stole. You thief.

SATAN: I didn't thieve anything [*folds hands on table, assured*] I think I want to be a construction worker.

KHHKR: [*pouring out more sugar*] I'm horny. I want you to fuck me a lot today. I mean, like you don't even know me. Will you fuck me like a stranger?

SATAN: [*nodding*] Yes I will. You mean like holding you down and screaming louder when you start to say 'ow'?

KHHKR: Yes, like that. Then we can sleep until the sun is gone [*laughs*]

They then take turns blowing and flicking sugar at each other. Snowflakes hit the window and melt. Full daylight. The construction workers return. They talk and point different directions down the roads. Their mouths are quiet, they are distanced. Muted.

SATAN: You're pretty.

KHHKR: Blah blah.

SATAN: No you're a pretty person.

He blows a hard breath and all the sugar goes onto Khhkr's lap. Then he surveys the other customers. A hideous woman some tables down is bringing a bite of pancakes to her mouth. And the syrup falls onto her sweatshirt. She looks down at the syrup, her neck folding out. She looks at the syrup, chewing. And Satan watches.

SATAN: [*playing with his straw*] I want to ask the hideous woman if she thinks about how many people are embarrassed by her presence [*lifting thumb from end of straw and letting water drop onto table in single drops*] I want to ask her if she worries about being immortal. That is, if she were immortal, exactly as she is right now, would it be agonizing? Is she having a good time? Is she really excited and happy about eating pancakes? Is this fun for her?

Satan turns back to Khhkr when he feels sugar particles rain on his lap.

KHHKR: Blah blah [*getting up*] Let's go.

A very pale, fat man with fetal alcohol syndrome works the register. Purple rings round out his eyes. He takes their bill and looks at it.

EMPLOYEE WITH FAS: Tank ewe.

KHHKR: [*staring at him, pointing*] You don't have any friends.

He smiles back.

KHHKR: [*evenly*] You don't know anyone that would willingly spend time with you, and that is because you are terrible. I am embarrassed standing in front of you. The way I am supposed to keep my opinion, my disgust towards you, covered. That seems wrong. I know how pathetic you feel [*tapping fingers on counter*] What do you do when you leave this place? You hang up your nametag and walk home, right. There is nothing at home that you want or care about and you only go there because you paid for it. Did you pay for it? Does your mom pay for it? Is your mom still alive? Did your mom love you? Have you ever thought you loved another human? Have you ever experienced happiness? Do you like to have change in your pockets or not? Did you enjoy buying the shirt or pants you are wearing? When you were in the dressing room, trying them on, did you silently celebrate? Do you enjoy having those glasses that like, get tinted when it gets dark?

Have you ever wanted to just run into a tree headfirst and sleep for a while? How many people have called you stupid to your face, and how many times have you openly agreed? How many times have you agreed quietly? If we were playing a board game, would you look at me or just look down at the pieces? Have you ever been up really late and thought to yourself, "How am I going to stay alive when I hate myself this much?" How many times would I have to hit you in the arm before you cried? Have you ever hurt someone's feelings and then regretted it? Or do you only get your feelings hurt, but then apologize for other people? [*nodding*] Yeah, that's you. That is you.

The employee with FAS leans over the counter on his elbows, and he looks at the bill. He tries to raise his glasses by twitching his nose. His shirt is way too big. His name is written on a plastic tag. And next to the register, there are some homemade cookies with smiley faces painted on them. A waitress comes out from the backroom and stands by the register. Khhkr grabs a smiley face cookie and slides it forward.

KHHKR: And one of these please.

EMPLOYEE WITH FAS: Hi. Tank ewe.

He points at the amount on the register and sniffs. Khhkr gets out her wallet and gives him a twenty, looking from the waitress to him.

KHHKR: You can keep the rest.

EMPLOYEE WITH FAS: Ok. Tank ewe.

Khhkr touches his hand.

KHHKR: [*softly*] Run away with me. Let's get married [*touches his chin*] I love you. Hey look at me. Look at me, I, love you. Leave with me. We can share everything. I'll make you happy. I promise. We can live on smiley face cookies.

EMPLOYEE WITH FAS: Ok. Ok tank ewe.

KHHKR: I'm average in a way more painful than being below-average.

WAITRESS: [*to Satan*] Your friend's an asshole.

SATAN: Yeah, but so are you. And me too. What's left? Are we done?

Satan smiles at both employees and takes a mint and leaves.

[*Later.*]

A small bathroom. Satan is cutting Khhkr's hair. She sits on a folding chair with a cape of old newspaper and he stands behind her. There are loud crunching clips.

SATAN: [*sprays her hair*] What kind of shampoo do you use? It's making me hard. Is it some kind of raspberry?

KHHKR: [*chin against chest*] There is only one kind of raspberry. [*pauses*] There is only one raspberry and it will dominate us all with its giant fists.

They both laugh.

SATAN: [*shaking some wet hairs off his fingers*] Now I am imagining you standing on a huge raspberry with nothing on but white socks. White socks that are kind of worn-looking and half pulled-off [*clips, shakes hair off fingers*] On the huge raspberry, you are smiling. Your legs are sinking into the raspberry and there are drops of juice on your knees. You are dying and sinking into the huge raspberry. It's ok though. You're smiling.

KHHKR: [*laughs*] You are imagining one mean-ass raspberry [*shivers, hair clippings hit Satan's feet, he shuffles*] Will you defend me from this mean-ass raspberry?

Satan snips his own knuckle.

SATAN: Fuck [*puts finger in mouth, spits out some hairs*] It depends.

There is silence. During the silence they both think about what it depends on. Clipping sounds.

SATAN: [*clears throat*] I still have the brownies you made when I first visited you [*combing her hair, clipping*] When I first went to your house I thought your house looked shitty from the outside. Like I thought an actual piece of shit would answer the door [*snips*] And I was right.

They both laugh.

KHHKR: [*still laughing*] Awww shit [*stops laughing, brushes nose with hand*] I made you the brownies because I thought you would interpret them as a bribe to leave and never come back. Like payment in advance [*wiggles toes, looks at them*] I figured we would set up a relationship in which I would leave brownies out on the front step and you would take them with the agreement that you were never to see me again. It didn't work out that way and you kept coming back. That's fine. It's fine. Blah blah. It's like Chad the Fly said.

SATAN: Who?

KHHKR: Chad the Fly, from the book I told you about. He was friends with the frog even though he knew the frog was going to eat him. He knew he was going to die. Chad the Fly said, "Friends are the dead bodies for the larva of relationships."

Satan lifts her hair. He looks at the back of her neck. He clips her hair then combs it. The quiets are very quiet.

SATAN: [*clears throat*] Don't turn around and look at me while I am saying this [*clips*] Ok?

KHHKR: [*pause*] Ok.

SATAN: When I got home that night—with the brownies—I took them out of the glass tray and wrapped them in an unfolded napkin. Then I put them in the fridge [*pause*] They're still there. I just can't throw them out. I can't throw out the brownies you made. You made them so good I think [*clips, shakes scissors off to the side*] Sometimes I open the fridge and think, "It's time to throw them out." And I even reach in like I am going to do it. But I don't. I never do. Really though—they're too nice. They're too nice to throw out. If those brownies were real people, I would like, take them to a dance or ask them out for dinner [*stops cutting*] The brownies, they are nice to have to look at when I can't help but notice that I am alone in my apartment—and I start thinking, what if that is the only nice thing anyone will ever do for me? Really though [*resumes cutting*] they're way too pretty. And now they're all thin and hard, wrapped in a napkin deep in the back of my fridge. I look at them every once in a while because I just can't throw them out. Or eat them. They're too pretty. Really. I think maybe something like that is impossible to explain [*puts a wet clipping in his pocket*] Tonight when the sun sets I will lay my head on the horizon and wait to be crushed. Don't come and get me. Don't come and sweep me up. Don't do anything except be the greatest [*laughs quickly*] Did Chad the Fly say anything about greatness.

KHHKR: Your fingers are cold [*shivers then straightens*] Cut my hair so close that it disappears and never comes back. I'm too pretty for you [*evenly*] Too fucking pretty.

SATAN: You could pretend I am hair and do that to me, if you want to. I'd let that happen.

Khhkr catches clippings in her overturned palms. She looks at them. Then turns her hands over and drops them.

KHHKR: From now on I want you to fuck me through the open zipper on my pants. Because I don't want to be naked in front of you.

They are quiet for the remainder of the haircut. After, they leave the bathroom and go to Satan's room, adjoining. Khhkr looks at herself in the window as a mirror. Behind her, Satan wipes the hair off the scissors, onto the ground.

KHHKR: I like my haircut. Thank you very much. I wouldn't have been able to do this myself.

SATAN: Good. You're welcome [*looks up at her*] You look like a little boy.

Satan rubs the hair into the carpet threads with his toes, still shaking the scissors off.

KHHKR: [*looks at him in window mirror*] We always have fun together.

Satan sets the scissors on the floor. Then he lies down on a pile of clothing he uses for a bed, in the corner of the small room.

SATAN: When you are not here I sleep on the couch downstairs. And I like to keep the television on. I can feel it against my neck when I turn my back. It feels good. I wake up when it's still dark out and sit on the tile floor in front of my tv, flicking the channels and pretty much just looking at things.

KHHKR: [*makes a kissy face to herself*] I am a failure and so are you.

SATAN: You look pretty though. Yeah. You do.

Khhkr goes to walk over to him but she steps on the scissors. The scissors cut her foot deep. She hisses. The ball of her left foot drips blood, and she holds it up knee-high for inspection. Satan takes her to the shower and cleans her foot off with cupped-handfuls, using the other hand to balance her at the hip.

KHHKR: [*hands on the showerwall*] Is it good?

SATAN: [*shuts faucet*] It's good yeah.

He dries her foot off with his shirt and puts a bandaid over the cut.

KHHKR: [*turning her head*] What's that on the bandaid?

SATAN: It's a duck giving a thumb's up.

Khhkr turns her head to the showerwall again.

KHHKR: [*flatly*] Does the duck look happy?

SATAN: Yes [*massaging her foot*] Yes I feel that this duck is happy. To be touching your blood, this duck is happy. Thumbs up.

KHHKR: [*puts foot down carefully*] Ok.

They go to bed. Khhkr falls asleep. Satan does not. He spends the first few minutes of the night sticking his tongue in and out at her. In between he quietly repeats, "This should hurt your feelings." But he never seems convinced it actually hurts her feelings. Keeps checking her face. Different angles. He takes the top blanket and goes downstairs to the kitchen. The kitchen is dark. Satan leans his elbows on the counter and looks outside. The moon is a toenail clipping in the sky.

SATAN: This kitchen is small and it is cold. Very cold. And I don't want to be here. That is all I need to know about this kitchen.

He sits on his couch in the next room. Stares at the television on the floor, not turned on.

SATAN: Maybe the roof will fall on me and kill me.

He looks up at the ceiling. He sits there waiting. Then he gets up and kneels on the tile. He turns the tv on and changes the channels, listless, finally landing on a high school basketball game. Each time the One Too-Loud Broadcaster says something, the Other Too-Loud Broadcaster says, "What?" Then there is static. Eventually, the first one says, "Jesus, nothing Jerry—forget it." Satan changes to the news. He imagines himself as the cloud he sees on the weather forecast, the one the meteorologist shows looming over the Midwest, wearing sunglasses and a smile. He imagines himself roaming low over the states, decimating everything. Trees uproot and fly into livingrooms, killing entire families, their dogs, destroying pictures, furniture, work-out equipment, and whatever else. Fathers outside with their sons, together they feel the opening drafts. "What is it father?" And with a stern look to the sky, the father says, "Nothing son—Goddamn it—it's nothing." Right before coalescing with other clouds wearing sunglasses. Smiling through the onslaught. Blowing entire states off the map like shingles, into the ocean without hesitation.

SATAN: [*yawning, watery-eyed*] Days are the worst thing ever made.

He goes to the refrigerator and opens it and looks at the brownies at the back of the fridge.

SATAN: There is no way I can throw them out. They're too pretty. Really though [*hesitates, then shuts door*]

He goes outside and stands on the sidewalk with the blanket wrapped around him, over his head. And he holds the blanket closed underneath his chin. It is freezing out. There's a sock near the gate of the apartment complex fence, frosted and stiffened to the ground.

SATAN: See you in the spring you lost sock. Who lost you, sock? You are lost. No one will want you again. Goodbye. See you in the spring, lost sock. I have nothing else to say. Lost sock, I can't help you. I'll see you later.

There are no construction workers in sight.

EZZARD AND FANON

A small kitchen connected to a livingroom. In the livingroom there's a couch, tv and washer/dryer along the wall. Ezzard sits on the couch. Fanon stands with his elbows on the counter in the kitchen, looking into the livingroom. They both have trouble with balance, and fall at random. The television on, sound off. There is a video on the news, captured by a bank security camera. On the video, a man walks down the sidewalk. The caption on the bottom of the screen says, "Down Syndrome Man Killed On Street."

EZZARD: [*still looking at tv*] Wait is 'Down Syndrome Man' how they're referring to someone or is that an action figure I don't know about? [*falls off couch, hits head on wall, gets back up*] Fuck.

FANON: [*holding counter to keep from falling*] Huh? [*ignores*] Hey I'm supposed to ask you something. My friend's looking to sell something. I'm supposed to ask you [*almost falls*] He's got a full deer spine, like all the vertebra or whatever. Do you know anyone who would want it? [*pause, swaying*] Would you?

In the video a white circle highlights another man, approaching Down Syndrome Man in a quiet run.

EZZARD: [*watching video*] Why would I want that?

Fanon holds onto the counter to keep from falling.

FANON: Why? [*pause, arms shaking on counter*] Uh you could, put a string through all the pieces and, hang it. You could keep evil away. I don't know [*changes tone*] I have poptarts too—they're old—but you want one, man?

On the news video, a man approaches Down Syndrome Man and swings a bat, hitting Down Syndrome Man in the head. The collision sends him to the sidewalk, face forward fast. And a black pool expands from his head. The security video loops back to the start. Ezzard watches, trying not to fall off the couch again.

EZZARD: [*touching face with both hands*] The way he hit the ground had to have scraped off part of his face. His face is gone for sure. Or at least part of it.

FANON: What?

EZZARD: [*didn't hear*] What will they do with that man's face? Did they get it out of the sidewalk? It has to be gone. What happened? Why am I watching this?

Fanon falls to the floor and hits his head on the tile. He shakes on the tile.

FANON: [*getting up*] Hey man. So you know anybody that'd want that deer spine. Also, did you want that poptart or no? You didn't answer that either. And I kind of want it. So.

The video on the news ends, loops back to the beginning. There is the bat, the fall, and again Down Syndrome Man's head blooming a black pool against the sidewalk.

EZZARD: [*staring at black pool*] No, I don't think so. I don't want them.

FANON: [*lights cigarette*] No you don't think you want the poptart, or no about the deer spine? We're not communicating effectively. I'm not blaming you, but I feel like my life is worth less than usual right now [*leans over the counter, coughing—puts head on his forearms and coughs, his finger up—then he squints through the kitchen light, trying to stay standing*] Damn, he nailed that retard.

Down Syndrome Man falls again. The black pool grows again. Ezzard and Fanon watch the looping video in silence.

EZZARD: [*staring at tv*] I don't want to leave because I am worried this house is in outer space and I'll die if I walk out the door.

FANON: [*tries to walk*] Alright, that's it [*swaying in the middle of the kitchen*] I'm going to eat the poptart then.

The video continues to loop in silence. Behind them in the livingroom, an old woman gets out of the dryer. She closes the dryer, then walks through the livingroom to the kitchen. She wears sweatpants tucked into dinosaur slippers. No shirt on. In the kitchen she takes a cookie from a plastic bin near the stove. She leans over the stove and bites the cookie, letting crumbs falls from her mouth to beneath the burners where all the other crumbs are already black. She walks back to the dryer and gets in. Ezzard and Fanon watch, swaying and falling over.

FANON: [*eating poptart, trying not to fall again*] All humans have faces and that's what makes them hard to hate.

EZZARD: For me, that's how I keep track of the ones I hate.

Fanon nods, chewing. He puts the last corner of the poptart in his mouth then ties the garbagebag together, removes it. He tries not to fall. The bottom of the bag rips and a can of spaghetti sauce hits the carpet. It leaves a huge stain.

EZZARD: [*swaying, falls hard*] Oh my God. What happened [*slowly, staring at stain*] What happened?

FANON: [*staring at stain*] I know. What happened?

Fanon takes an aerosol can out of the cabinet and sprays carpet-cleaning foam on the stain. The foam expands.

FANON: [*watching the foam expand, his hands on his knees*] Look, it's a cloud.

EZZARD: [*watching too, hands on knees*] Yes it's very pretty.

FANON: Yes, it is very pretty. I need to eat part of that cloud [*reconsidering*] I want to at least. Seeing that I have lived this long without eating part of a cloud, I don't think I really need to. I probably just want to.

EZZARD: Yes [*falls, stands slowly*] Do it. I want to see that. Eat part of it. Come on. It's too nice not to eat. And I'm not hungry. You eat it.

Fanon kneels down and scoops pieces of the cloud out with his tongue and he eats them. He cringes, but keeps eating.

FANON: [*swallowing away the burning feeling*] It feels good in my belly. I like that it's there. There are people having picnics in my stomach. And the people having picnics are getting their shade now. And they are thanking me [*nodding, looking at floor*] Yeah this feels good.

EZZARD: [*swaying*] Their shade never comes.

Fanon doesn't respond. He stares at the carpet. The muscles move around in his face as he grinds his teeth and jaw, staring at the foam but not really noticing it. He takes slow breathes in an attempt to avoid vomiting.

EZZARD: [*pointing at foam*] It is still the same size. It's like we're not here. Why is it ignoring us? [*loudly*] There is no way to control it. What should we do?

FANON: [*exhales, audibly*] The cloud is bigger than both of us. There is no way to kill it. [*falls face-first into foam, pushes himself up slowly*]

EZZARD: [*kneeling too*] Keep trying. Please. Keep eating it; it has to get smaller. It will get smaller if you keep eating it. Just keep trying.

FANON: [*gags, eyes water*] When the cloud is all gone, we will forget why we wanted it gone.

EZZARD: I don't care at all. Just do what I told you to do.

They stare, on hands and knees, watching the cloud to see if it will keep getting bigger. A group of people enters the room, from down the hall. The people go to sleep on the floor.

EZZARD: [*standing and trying not to fall*] I think I'm going to leave now. I am not scared of stepping into outer space anymore. It doesn't matter.

Ezzard steps over someone now sleeping on the floor. And a few steps in departure, Fanon pushes him into the wall. His body goes halfway into the wall. And dust powders the floor.

FANON: [*hiccups, winces*] I'm sorry. I am really sorry. I mean that [*gags, coughs*] It must've been something I ate. It must've been the cloud I ate. I don't know why I did that. I'm sorry [*extends his hand*] Seriously.

Ezzard removes himself from the wall, wincing. Holding his limp arm.

EZZARD: That's ok. I understand.

FANON: Will you help me fix the wall at least? [*in sing-song*] I'll-be-nice [*puts hands up*] I won't do anything mean again. Swear to God.

PERSON SLEEPING ON FLOOR: [*back turned*] Keep it fucking down.

ANOTHER PERSON SLEEPING ON THE FLOOR: Seriously.

EZZARD: [*touching bruised arm*] I will help you. Because I don't want the indentation of my body to be here forever.

They leave, and return with a piece of drywall and a saw. More people come in and sleep.

FANON: Hold it while I cut [*loudly, face close to Ezzard*] Hold it fucking still [*shakes the drywall*]

He runs the saw along the drywall and accidentally cuts into the webbing of Ezzard's thumb and forefinger. The saw sinks in two rubbery pulls, very deep.

EZZARD: [*pulls away, looks at ragged bluish cut*] Wait [*coughs*] Hold on.

FANON: [*looking at Ezzard's bloody hand*] I'm sorry. I didn't mean to do that. I apologize to you [*swaying*]

EZZARD: It's ok. I understand

He lifts his foot and, using his sock, tries to clean bloodstain off the new drywall. His hand drips to the floor and onto the sleeping people.

EZZARD: [*falls, stands*] Let's just finish this. Let's just finish this so I can leave.

They finish fitting the drywall. The border is apparent, and in the middle of the new segment, a red stain smeared in a smoky blotch.

EZZARD: [*seeing stain on the wall*] I think I am going to go now even though I might be stepping into outerspace. Bye.

FANON: [*lifting foot from between sleeping people*] I'll go with you. I don't want to be here [*almost falls over a sleeping body*] Wait.

Ezzard and Fanon leave through the front door, walking over the people sleeping on the floor. They walk to a middleschool playground. The middle school's sign says: "Hav a g eat summr every1"

EZZARD: [*getting on swing*] Hav a geat summr.

FANON: I will, I promise [*beginning to swing*] Hey, give me an underdog. Do you know how to do an underdog?

EZZARD: [*jumps off the swing, falls*] I certainly do sir.

FANON: [*head slightly turned*] Don't touch me though. I won't like that. Even if it's an accident.

After three pushes Ezzard stops and sits in the woodchips, watching Fanon reach up with his feet. In the middle of the playground area there's an abandoned sandal, with a cartoon rhino on the front. The sandal is dirty and ripped. Ezzard watches it as Fanon starts to tell a joke. Halfway through the joke, Ezzard stops paying attention. He rubs his ear, wincing a little. Then he laughs when a pause suggests Fanon is expecting him to laugh.

EZZARD: I wish that when they left the house earlier that it was outerspace. Although [*pause*] maybe it was.

FANON: Huh? [*swinging high*] Faces are how I keep track of the humans I like. And smiling is how I keep track of the faces I have not failed.

EZZARD: [*kicking woodchips at sandal*] Smiling is fantastic and wonderful, but sometimes it is too much.

FANON: [*looking up at sky*] So you don't want that deer spine? How will you keep the evil away?

EZZARD: No I don't want the evil to be an orphan [*grabs ankles and crosses legs*] I don't.

Quiet. There is a little wind. And they let themselves become part of the giant background that includes the rest of material objects—not different. Neither of them fight it. They sit and enjoy it.

THE BASTARDS [THEY MAKE A HOLOCAUST]

An apartment. A male ghost and a female ghost are sitting on a couch in the livingroom. They are not looking at each other. There is a hallway off the side.

MALE GHOST: Where is the younger, less self-sufficient human? I am becoming jealous of him because he is receiving more attention from you than I am. He gets to have you as his mommy for a little bit. Where is he? I want to see if he is superior to me and worthy of your attention. Can we burn him? Where is he?

FEMALE GHOST: [*scratching her knee*] He's in his room playing with blocks. He imagines that he makes the blocks into things. He told me he builds cities and when he can see every face in the city, he rolls over it all. He told me that before you came over. Before you came over, he was being a very nice boy to me.

MALE GHOST: [*looking at her, serious*] We should kill him. [*pauses, puts his hand on her leg*] I mean it. I'm jealous. You are too important to me for me to lose. I don't want to lose you. Please.

With hand still on her knee, the male ghost kneels.

FEMALE GHOST: [*avoiding eye contact*] No, we can't do that. I mean I thought about it but I'm supposed to be watching him, making sure he is safe. That would be the opposite. Do you understand that? [*staring at him*] It just came to me earlier [*combs the male ghost's hair with her fingers*] Sucks I know. But I have to be his mommy for a little bit.

MALE GHOST: [*looks around, pauses*] We should teach him about ghosts then yeah? [*tapping her legs with his open hands, soft*] Otherwise, he won't know about them. If he doesn't know about them, he will fear them [*face of unfortunate reason*] And since they are everywhere—well he'd be afraid all the time. I really think we should. I really think yeah?

FEMALE GHOST: Well, first [*she stops combing his hair*] My hug meter is low. My hug meter is dangerously low—and, I just wish I knew someone who could help me.

The male ghost leans up to her, his waist between her legs. They hug, her on the couch, him still kind of kneeling. The hug is annoying to them both.

FEMALE GHOST: I lied. I don't have a hug meter. You're fucking stupid [*her finger jabbing his cheek*] You don't know anything about ghosts [*still jabbing*] Who taught you? Who taught you huh? [*her face is close to his now*] You, are in my control.

The male ghost pushes her fingers and face away. Then he stands.

MALE GHOST: There is no such thing as a mutual hug. You taught me that [*dismissive*] Now, let's teach the younger, less self-sufficient human about ghosts. He will thank us.

The male ghost extends his hand and the female ghost puts hers around it.

FEMALE GHOST: [*smiles and nods*] We will teach the younger less self-sufficient human about ghosts [*stands*] Maybe he will not thank us. But that is ok. You shouldn't get thanked for everything you do. You should just do things.

MALE GHOST: [*smells her hand*] Thank you for another lesson.

They go into an adjoining room and return with sheets. They scissor out eyeholes and dress each other with the sheets, adjusting the eyeholes while laughing. The sheets make their voices sound static-thin, as if produced by an old radio. And they do test sounds and they look at each other, unable to recognize anything through the eyeholes. Then they hug again.

MALE GHOST: [*static, tinny*] There is no such thing as mutual hug.

FEMALE GHOST: [*sheet blowing outward with her breaths*] Do I look like a ghost? You think I'm ready?

MALE GHOST: [*static*] Yes. How about me? Do I? [*arms out, looking down*] I feel like I look stupid. Do I look like a ghost or what? Or just stupid.

FEMALE GHOST: Yes absolutely.

They walk down the hall to a room where a boy is playing with blocks. He's wearing a shirt with a smiling helicopter on the front.

And there's a city on the floor, made of blocks and he is preparing to roll over it. But the door opens. And it swishes the carpet. Two ghosts stand in the doorway, saying nothing. Sound of heavy static breathing.

FEMALE GHOST: [*static thin*] What are you making?

The boy sits up. Is still. And he pinches his toes, avoiding eye contact. He avoids looking into the eyeholes. An ant climbs the tallest building in the city and looks around. Another small bug, one that looks like a fish with antennae walks up a building too.

MALE GHOST: [*nose shaking the tented sheet, static*] Is it a city?—Huh? It looks so nice [*breathing loud*] Are you going to let that fish-bug move in? How about me? Let us into your neighborhood yeah?

BOY: [*still pinching toes*] Why do them bugs like to live in my hair?

FEMALE GHOST: Yeah [*coming into room*] It's nice. I like it. Let me in too, let me move into your city.

BOY: [*distracted*] Yeah.

They all ignore each other, in favor of staring at the ant and the bug resembling a fish, both on top of the buildings.

MALE GHOST: Whoa I really like it. Can I rent a room in one of the buildings? Or has this fish-bug guy here already claimed everything?

There is a long pause.

BOY: [*to no one*] Why do them bugs like to live in my hair.

The female ghost approaches closer, and touches the back of the boy's neck. He flicks a block idly and shudders. Bumps populate his neck.

FEMALE GHOST: Yeah, everyone gets to live in the city.

BOY: [*urgent, loud*] No.

FEMALE GHOST: No? Why not?

BOY: Just because.

Then both ghosts are touching the back of the boy's neck, together at the same time. With thin static-laughing they rub their hands over him and he is menaced.

MALE GHOST: [*facing her*] I like this.

FEMALE GHOST: Me too. It feels so good.

MALE GHOST: Well then. Let's keep doing it yeah?

FEMALE GHOST: Let's.

MALE GHOST: [*looking down*] What about this one? [*touches a building, sending it swaying*] This one looks nice. Can I move into this one? [*laughing*]

The male ghost keeps touching buildings, as well as the boy's neck. And the female ghost laughs, steps back. She observes the touching.

FEMALE GHOST: [*clapping hands once*] You two make such a pair!

Both ghosts laugh at the boy. And touch him and his buildings freely.

BOY: [*upset*] No.

MALE GHOST: [*knocks building over*] This one right here?

BOY: [*screaming*] Don't touch it.

MALE GHOST: Sorry. I'm sorry. You want me to leave don't you? Just tell me. Don't you? If you want me to leave just tell me [*tone then friendlier*] But if you sit there, I will stay [*taps boy's head*] I will stay exactly where I am then. Me and the fish-bug here will split an apartment in the city. I hope we don't fight over dishes or something yeah? Don't roll over us yeah?

The boy backs up and tries to hide underneath his steel bedframe, whining from both. He tugs the toe area of the socks he's wearing, lying sideways under the bedframe.

BOY: Get out.

The ghosts kneel by the bedframe and stare beneath. They reach in and keep touching the boy's face and neck. They put their hands all over his face, pressing hard.

FEMALE GHOST: Remember [*blowing the sheet with heavy breathing*] no one will be your enemy like we will. That is my promise. Pinky swear.

She puts her head underneath the bedframe and presses her head into the boy, very hard. She repeats, "No one will be your enemy like we will" over and over, saying it the same way each time.

MALE GHOST: No one [*reaching under bed*] The younger generations breath our last breaths. That's what a ghost is. When can I move in? Huh? When can me and the fish-bug move in with all our stuff?

He puts his head underneath the bed too, next to the female's. Both ghosts lean in closer and breathe onto the boy's face. Touching everywhere. And the boy fights out through their hands and exits the room running. As the ghosts take theirs heads out from under the bed there is a loud fall from down the hallway. Then wet screaming. The ghosts find the boy on the tile floor in the bathroom, his lip split open. Blood streaks the bathtub and the tile too. The female ghost sits on the toilet, lifting the boy to her lap. He is already pale, his face curled into a raw frown, reddened—the upper lip split through to the teeth, reaching up to the lower left eyelid. He screams. The female ghost grabs his lips and holds them shut with her fingers. There is struggle. Bubbles comes from his screaming mouth, down his chin. And the male ghost watches, distractedly touching a stick of antiperspirant left by the sink. He notices his hand on the antiperspirant.

MALE GHOST: I heard you're not supposed to use antiperspirant. I heard it's supposed to be bad for you.

Blood trails the female ghost's arm. She looks at the male ghost.

FEMALE GHOST: How is it bad.

MALE GHOST: Like that's what I read.

FEMALE GHOST: [*struggling harder*] Where did you read that.

MALE GHOST: Actually, I don't know.

FEMALE GHOST: Call the parents [*pause, struggling*] He is theirs. They are the ones who love him and they are the ones who need to know. The number's on the fridge. They will want to know of the change he has undergone.

MALE GHOST: [*still wobbling the antiperspirant*] I don't really feel like talking to anyone right now though. Can I just leave them a note? That would be easier for me. If you don't mind. Can I do that? Do you mind me doing that?

Before the female ghost can answer, she secures a different hold on the boy's mouth, using a section of the sheet for traction. Pathetic screaming in between. There is a large amount of blood on her sheet and she is very strong.

MALE GHOST: It's just that I don't feel like talking right now though.

FEMALE GHOST: That's fine [*looks at the boy*] I accept that. Do whatever you want.

The male ghost nods for a period of time after everyone is done speaking. He stares at the screaming face, as it lisps from the split. Bloodstains have triumphed the boy's shirt too. The helicopter on his shirt is covered in blood.

MALE GHOST: [*staring at shirt*] And the helicopter continues to smile.

FEMALE GHOST: [*trying to hold the squirming boy*] The helicopter is a lesson in adversity. If only we could all learn to be more like the helicopter.

MALE GHOST: Yes.

She struggles to keep the boy's lips pinched, but blood has wetted things entirely. The male ghost stands in it. He seems confused.

FEMALE GHOST: Look at me. I'm a ventriloquist [*snaps with her free hand*] I always knew it. Don't you just want to paralyze me? Aren't I just the sexiest?

The male ghost stares at her, moving his toes over the pooled floor.

MALE GHOST: Boo to you both [*points at the boy*] You missed a spot.

FEMALE GHOST: [*points at the male ghost*] I missed a spot.

MALE GHOST: And the helicopter continues to smile.

They both laugh. The male ghost goes to the kitchen and finds paper and a pencil. He writes the note.

THE NOTE: Just to get right to it here—your younger, less self-sufficient human is bleeding. He split his mouth on the tub. I don't know what's going on. But he totally ruined the shirt he's wearing. It's the one with the smiling helicopter on it. The helicopter seems fine. Bye. Sincerely, all the people you plan on never seeing again.

The male ghost returns to the bathroom. The female ghost is holding the boy down, his head against the tile. He hacks uncontrollably as hands hold his face. Everything is red. The bathroom is warm grossness.

FEMALE GHOST: You know what [*looking at the wound*] I think we can fix it real quick. We can fix it and then leave so we don't have to talk to the people who own him. They will be impressed with our responsibility [*shrugging*] Everyone wins. Right?

MALE GHOST: Ok [*steps more into bathroom*] You got it boss.

The female ghost takes a pin from the drawer and pulls out a few of her hairs through the eyehole of the sheet. Then she tries to thread the hair and sew back together the boy's lips, while the male ghost holds the boy down. The hairs break when she tries to pull them through. Everything is sticky and spread.

MALE GHOST: [*struggling to hold bloody-lips closed*] His face is all uneven now. No one will find him attractive [*sullenly*] We set out to teach him one thing, and we failed. We fucking failed. Should we go get some scissors and make his face into one of those snowflake things where you fold a piece of paper in half them unfold it into a beautiful symmetrical snowflake? How about that? Do you know what I am talking about? Everyone likes those things [*defiantly*] Who doesn't like those things? But maybe that would help him yeah? [*toneless, looking at floor*] I don't know what's going on.

FEMALE GHOST: Alright [*trying to peel hairs off her fingers*] fuck it. I'm done. I won't be able to hold him down while you cut him with scissors. That will be too painful for him. Let's just leave. I'm annoyed and bored and I lack confidence in this whole effort. Let's just leave.

They leave the boy on the floor of the bathroom, still screaming and mutilated. They sit on the couch in the livingroom again. And they remain quiet, not facing each other. And the quiet seems part of the room. They can scoop it out with their hands if they want to save themselves, but neither of them want to. So they don't.

EVERYONE WANTS TO WORK AT THE CLOUD FACTORY

At midday a person pulls his car up to a fastfood drive-thru, braking by the speaker. He looks at the car radio, no expression as he turns it down. In the distance there are refineries lining the horizon. He stares at the rows of refineries, seems lost. Turns back to speaker when it scratches.

THE SPEAKER: Hi can I take your order?

PERSON: Yeah—You sure can. But first, I need you to hold on, please. Just hold on.

THE SPEAKER: [*static*] Ok, take your time [*static*] We'll get through this together.

PERSON: We will. And I promise, I'll take my time.

THE SPEAKER: [*static*] Good to hear.

The person surveys the menu. He feels hurried and wonders about the appropriate length of time to make a choice. Then he considers how much time he is adding to the process by considering it. The words on the menu lose meaning in the panic, and he opts for the pictures.

PERSON: [*to himself*] They should have three-dimensional pictures so people can imagine the actual size [*pause*] What am I doing?

On the display there is a picture of another person his age enjoying a chicken sandwich.

PERSON: Alright, hello?

THE SPEAKER: [*static*] Yes sir, what can I get for you?

PERSON: I read that your Spicy Chicken Sandwich will take me "South of the border." Is that true?

THE SPEAKER: One Spicy Chicken for the man in the fucking sweet Camry. Anything else?

PERSON: No, I'm not trying to order one yet, I was just curious if I will be mysteriously transported to Mexico or South America somewhere, because I'd need to know in advance to let someone know to get my mail for me and prevent the newspapers from accumulating in front of my door.

THE SPEAKER: [*static*] You won't be transported. Would you like a Spicy Chicken or no?

PERSON: Well [*shifts to park*] hold on. That changes things. [*pauses*] I'm confused about where we're at in the process now. Can I just pull around again so it's like a do-over? So it's like we never met?

A long silence follows. The person takes a deep breath and rubs his head slowly, in becoming lost to the humming of his car's engine. He doesn't know what he has just said. Looks out the windshield into the distance, where the refineries at the end of the town emit smoke, and blend to clouding.

THE SPEAKER: [*static*] Sir? What can I get for you?

No answer. The person is still removed. He becomes aware again in a slow volley.

THE SPEAKER: What can I get for you.

PERSON: [*to back of car as if people are there*] Uh, I didn't order the Rude Sandwich [*then aloud*] Alright, how about this, the #6? It says it's, "Exploding with taste." Is that accurate? [*watches his mouth in the rearview mirror*] Exploding. Exploding.

THE SPEAKER: It is pretty good. Super good, Sir. Good in a big way, explodingly big taste. I'm fucking half-dead just thinking about it. Do you understand? [*screams*] Huh? [*then tonelessly*] I am imagining my exploded trunk bleeding into the dirt after having tasted the sandwich. The sandwich touches my mouth, and then I burst. Look around you, the parking lot should be hot with explosion remnants. The sandwich is amazing. [*static*]

PERSON: But—

THE SPEAKER: But no, you won't actually explode.

PERSON: I don't have to worry about my head bursting into pieces all over my car? Tell me that.

THE SPEAKER: No Sir.

PERSON: [*watching own mouth again*] And would you clean up the stains in my car if that happened?

THE SPEAKER: [*static*] I would do that for you, yes. I would clean the remains of your head off your car.

PERSON: Ok [*puts hands on steering wheel, turns it side to side*] Because, it would be pointless to buy the sandwich if I am going to die.

THE SPEAKER: Good point, Sir. I'll fix the menu so nobody else has to live in fear [*static*] You've done a brave thing. You deserve that fucking sweet Camry.

PERSON: [*not listening*] And the Radical Ranch Dippers?—How radical are they exactly? Tell me that.

THE SPEAKER: [*static*] Let me check [*shuffling sounds*] Ok—here it is, Radical Ranch Dippers. They have twice the amount of radical of most other places. Our team of scientists has discovered an extraction of radical, from a sample found deep within the earth's core.

PERSON: Polysaturated-radical or what?

THE SPEAKER: Yes to both [*static*]

Behind the Camry, another car honks. And the person drives away, in an awkward heave, forgetting that his brake is on. He leaves the shopping area and takes the side roads out, touring the town. He smiles at recognizable things, things that immediately recall an entire structure of feeling, himself very small in relation to it but also very much in control. The town is average. It begins to rain. The person enters a subdivision.

PERSON: I am ok.

He smiles and waves at the subdivision entrance sign. On the sign there's a lake painted there, and two genderless people in front of it, their faces gone from chipping. There is a green penis spraypainted going into one of their heads. The person nods hello to the wooden people as he turns in, passing the front lawn of the first house. Then more houses stacked in long rows.

PERSON: There can't be anyone in these houses. These houses are just stones that have ended up here. I am lost and scared [*watching mirror and road alternately*] Exploding. Exploding.

He drives around, talking incomplete sentences to himself. Rain still, but not as hard. Eventually he pulls over in front of someone's house and watches himself say "Exploding" for a few minutes. This seems to satisfy him. He gets out and leaves the car on the shoulder, still running. And he walks, watching his feet. He walks until he can't hear his car anymore. Sees a drainage grill along the curb. And there he takes out his driver's license, apartment keys and everything else in his pocket, including a roll of generic Lifesavers candy almost 2/3 full. And throws it all into the drainage grill. For a moment there's the water's hiss below. Then the things he's dropped, they splash. And he sits on the curb—elbows on his knees, hands on back of neck, watching the water go into the drain, carrying small tree branches, and birds, bugs, leaves, pieces of whatever, whatever is weaker than the current. The refineries are only blocks away, and he stares at them.

[*Later. Same scene.*]

A car parks down the road, same model and color as the person's. And a crossing guard exits. She begins crossing kids and buses when they come. In between, she approaches the person. He is wet, and sitting in the grass.

CROSSING GUARD: Hey—are you waiting for someone?

PERSON: [*not looking*] No.

CROSSING GUARD: Just sitting?

There is a pause.

PERSON: [*with weird relief*] Yeah, just sitting [*then, evenly*] I am just sitting.

CROSSING GUARD: Ok [*thumb over shoulder towards car*] If you want to come sit in my car with me—it's warm in there. Plus you can pick the radio setting. You can pick any station or kind of music but you can't have any of the carrots I brought because I only brought enough considering myself. I have a Camry [*thumb over shoulder towards car*] It's lovely.

The crossing guard keeps her thumb towards the Camry. And the person looks at the license plate. Seems speechless.

CROSSING GUARD: [*thumb still over shoulder*] That's my Camry you're looking at. It's lovely.

PERSON: I have a Camry too. It is lovely, you're right. When I sit inside it, I am in love [*watching a worm spasm on the street*] I want to sit next to you in your Camry and scratch your face really hard.

He leans forward and picks the worm up. Then he examines it, in its state still wet and knobbed with pieces of dirt. He sets the worm back into the grass. Another school bus passes, parting the street into miniature waves. The person waves to the staring kids. They frown at him. One does that, "you're crazy/finger around the head" thing, but without the accompanying "crazy face," just a stare.

CROSSING GUARD: None of them like you.

PERSON: The ridicule is unbearable. And the urge to fall down and cry is hard to resist.

He gets up and the crossing guard walks him to the car. In the car they sit together in silence. The heater is on.

PERSON: [*squinting against the heater*] I'm not worried about anything. I'm not confused.

CROSSING GUARD: [*takes out bag of carrots*] Sometimes when I'm alone in my room I just walk around in circles and look at the garbage on my floor. I'm always worried about falling and hitting my head on something and then not being able to get up. It seems really upsetting that another human would have to come in and find me dead like that [*eats carrot, optimistic*] But someone will have to I guess.

The person pats the crossing guard's shoulder. Then kisses her on the cheek. And beneath the kissed spot, a bruising forms on her cheek and eye orbital.

CROSSING GUARD: [*touches bruising*] No one has kissed me like that before. That gently [*eats carrot*] Thank you.

PERSON: I'm surprised anyone has ever kissed you. That seems unlikely.

CROSSING GUARD: [*rubs eye with hand holding bag of carrots*] Other people have kissed me.

PERSON: [*turns, watches refineries emit smoke far away*] I believe you I guess.

CROSSING GUARD: Nobody will ever forgive us on earth.

PERSON: I'm not worried about anything.

Neither continues. And the person leaves the car. He walks. He passes homes with quiet lawns, plastic toys on the sidewalks and birds lined up on the telephone wires. He ends up at a supermarket in a strip mall. He walks around the supermarket, not looking at anything. He grabs a can of tomato juice and an orange. He seems confused.

EMPLOYEE: Excuse me sir?

An employee greets him from behind a stand. She's handing out free samples. In front of her are crackers and some kind of dip. The person stops in front of the free sample stand.

EMPLOYEE: Would you like to try a free sample? They're delicious. I'm also willing to act like I am interested in your welfare, perhaps by attempting a discussion with you about something vague but relatable. We don't have to reveal anything important about ourselves. That would never happen anyway [*smiles beneath her green plastic visor*] It's like, a cheese spread with wine in it [*undoes her clasped hands and gestures*] Would you like a cracker, sir? Would you like me to teach you how to soundlessly murder an infant sir? My husband won't have sex with me. He masturbates in the bathroom and acts like he's brushing his teeth. But it doesn't take that long to brush your teeth. I know it doesn't take that long. Sometimes I try to check his boxers when he is sleeping, to see if they are stained. But I can't tell. Plus he would probably say that the stain was toothpaste. It's upsetting that I am married and in love with a fucking liar and a sneaky masturbator.

PERSON: "Sneaky masturbator" sounds like a cartoon villain I don't want to meet.

EMPLOYEE: [*stops smiling*] Oh you're gross [*pause*] Absolutely gross. You were born nine months after your mother swallowed her first genuine feeling of hatred towards her own life.

PERSON: I'm sorry [*looks at samples*] I don't know what I did wrong.

They stare at the free samples, ugly and uncomfortable under the lights. Very ugly.

EMPLOYEE: It's fine. Forget it. Let's talk about something else [*straightens her sign, different tone, not completely sincere*] I can't wait to get out tonight. It's supposed to be nice out tomorrow. I think I'm going to go to the park with my husband and bring some sandwiches. I like to lie in the grass and put the wet dandelions behind my ear—not the dry seedy ones [*fixing her bra strap*] Sometimes I forget to take them out from behind my ear and my husband and I wake up to find them all over in different places on the bed. He gets mad when that happens. He says he's worried about them staining the sheets. Fuck him. Fuck him in his stupid asshole.

The person sets the can and the orange on the stand. Then he rigidly holds out his cupped-hand. The employee hums to herself and spreads room temperature cheese on a cracker. Her knife breaks the cracker.

EMPLOYEE: Ah [*making fist*] I always fucking break the fucking thing. Here [*drops another into his hands, whispering*] Bullshit.

She eats the broken cracker and he eats his. And they make sure not to look at each other while eating. Somewhere in the avoidance, the person squints and coughs violently, spreading crumbs and some kind of cheese onto the display, and the employee's face also. The employee stands unmoving, unblinking.

PERSON: [*hand to his mouth ready to stifle the next spray*] It's good [*coughs and retches hard*] Good combination. The crumbs are on my tonsils.

He grabs the can and the orange and walks away coughing, red-faced and retching. There's a girl working the front register, blowing bubbles from a plastic wand she keeps in a container of bubble solution next to her. She affects customer recognition, finishing a row of bubbles from the wand. Then she rings up the tomato juice and the orange.

GIRL AT REGISTER: Can I see your ID?

PERSON: I have to show you my ID?

GIRL AT REGISTER: No I just want to see it [*blows another stream of bubbles*] I'm not lying. For some reason I just want to see your ID. [*stream of bubbles stops, she dunks the wand again*]

He hands her his ID. The girl looks at it, then back at him.

GIRL AT REGISTER: You look different.

PERSON: How so 'different'?

The girl watches him, alternating between the ID and his face. She dips the plastic wand in the bubble solution and blows some more bubbles. Some hit his face, and explode in lazy sequence. He puts his fingers to his face.

GIRL AT REGISTER: Different—like—you've been buried for a while [*hands ID back*] But only a little bit. Only a little bit buried. Relax—two, three weeks at most. Relax [*another stream of bubbles, tries to catch them in her hand*] Your driver's license contains the ghost of a very old you. A very old you that you can recall by name. Care to try our Super-Savers pick of the day? It's fresh cantaloupe.

PERSON: I'm sending you to hell in my mind.

GIRL AT REGISTER: Good because I don't know how to get there by myself.

PERSON: [*looking at driver's license*] The fastest way to hell is to stand still.

GIRL AT REGISTER: Forever sir [*eyebrows up*] So no cantaloupe?

PERSON: When I was buried for that little while, I told the worms that you're not far behind [*pause*] Relax, like two or three weeks.

GIRL AT REGISTER: [*sending more bubbles into his face*] I was hoping you did.

The person takes his purchases and leaves the store. He walks on the gravel shoulder of a road as the day gets darker. And he finds a place to sit on a dirt incline beneath an overpass. Holding the can and the orange, he looks out at the refineries emitting smoke, less than half a mile away. He imagines the refineries are cloud factories, and that he is employed there. Every day, he punches in and throws a huge lever—activating the machines that make clouds for the sky. And underneath the overpass he puts his head on the dirt. The coolness bites through his hair, touching his skull. He opens the can and drinks.

THE PERSON: [*watching the refinery smoke*] No one is ever going to miss me.

He drops the can and it rolls down the dirt into the street, where it spills against the gravel. He opens the orange with his thumbnail. The orange is filled with seeds, resembling tiny skulls. And he imagines the shape of the animal possessing skulls this shape. He sees the skulls take on bodies and walk over him, eating his body very slowly. It does not hurt. He flips out the tiny skulls in watery pops. They fall down the dirt incline. At the bottom of the dirt incline there's a puddle. Floating through the puddle there's a dead bird. The person wants to get up and feed the dead bird all the tiny skulls from the orange. But he is too tired. He remains there, watching the cloud factory on the surface of the puddle along the streetside.

BE NICE TO EVERYONE [VERSION 3]

Night. In an empty grocery store parking lot, a man and a woman sit in an idling car. He is young and she is old. They are sharing a cigarette. He sits in the passenger seat and she sits in the driver's seat. And they look out the windshield at the snow, both front windows down.

WOMAN: [*scratching eyebrow with pinkynail*] Did you ever play tag at recess? Did you play that a lot?

The man takes the cigarette from her fingers.

MAN: Yes. Yes I did.

WOMAN: [*slowly*] It's making me happy to think about tag right now. I always liked playing tag. That's a fun game. Isn't it?

MAN: [*staring out the windshield in a tired trance*] In tag there's only one loser at a time. And that loser is usually the slowest person. And the slowest person will try to look for another person to tag, but the only people they can catch are people that get hurt or have to tie their shoe or they trip. Ultimately it's hopeless. There will always be one loser at the end. There has to be a loser for that game to work.

WOMAN: No it works because there doesn't have to be a loser.

The woman turns on the windshield wiper and erases a few pieces of snow. She takes the cigarette back. Takes a pull, idly.

WOMAN: It's cold outside and I don't feel like doing anything. We should sit in this car until the snow piles up around it and we are buried. Will you stay here with me and get buried in snow? [*adjusts the heater, looks at him*] Do you want to do that? Do you want to wait here with me until we are buried in snow?

The man is still looking out the windshield in a tired trance.

MAN: No—that scares me. I don't want to do that.

The woman takes another pull, then puts the cigarette back between his fingers.

WOMAN: Why? [*speaking out the smoke*] You want to come sleep in my bed with me then? We can do that too.

The man comes out of his tired trance. He shivers and coughs. When he coughs he tastes something, grimaces. He swallows and coughs again.

MAN: No I'd rather go home and go to bed. By myself. My stomach hurts. I don't feel good. Fucking awful actually. I'd rather go home.

WOMAN: Why don't you just come home and sleep with me? I have a big warm bed [*pauses*] Our only options are getting buried in snow or sleeping in my bed. Which one sounds good to you right now? Hmm?

She looks at him. He stares at his hand on the window trim.

MAN: No, I don't think I want to do that. I don't want to sleep in your bed with you [*takes pull from cigarette*] No offense. But it blisters me to think of that. Please, I don't want that to happen. Promise me.

WOMAN: Why not? Just, come back and sleep with me. It's nothing. You'll like it. Blisters are just small happinesses trying to leave you. It's nothing. We can fix those. It's nothing.

MAN: [*after coughing again*] It is nothing. But I want to sleep by myself.

The woman begins to scratch the back of his neck. She studies his face.

WOMAN: Tag [*watching her own hand on his neck*] I think it'd be nice to sleep together. If anyone tried to kill you while you slept, I would be there to help you. You know I could defend you, you know. You know? Are you still nervous? I'm ready [*pause*] I'm ready. I'm a knife that's so sharp I never actually touch the ground, I keep falling through things. You know? [*smiles*] Tag.

MAN: [*turning from his stare*] Which way is it to my place? I'm just going to walk. I can walk it. I'm going.

WOMAN: [*quietly*] It'd be nice to go to my place and sleep in my bed, together. I have such a big bed. It's nice. Just once. Please come with me.

He backs away from her hand.

MAN: [*turns to window*] How do I get home?

Shivering, he drops the cigarette. The cigarette falls to the wet floormat.

WOMAN: It's awful to sleep alone—a lot awful.

The man sits up in his seat.

MAN: [*thoughtfully*] I don't know. I like to stretch my legs and arms out. That kind of behavior is incompatible with two people in one bed. Plus, my dick looks like a burnt match. Actually, I have a disease so bad I can't even think of what it is called or how to continue this lie. So you don't want that [*turns slowly to her, speaking slow, soft*] Haha when the burnt match fucks you, you will have a belly full of disgusting smoke and it will hurt. It will hurt in a way that makes you think, "Nothing has hurt before."

She ignores him, frowning, looking out the windshield at the snow.

WOMAN: It's awful to sleep alone. Awful. Why do you want to sleep in a bed small enough for only you? [*teasing*] If you had a choice there would be walls around your bed.

MAN: I heard you.

WOMAN: [*lowers heater*] I think it'd be nice to sleep together. There's nothing worse than thinking you have to be friends with someone and then trying too hard. I'm doing that with you and I think you're doing that with me [*reaches out and touches his shoulder*] Tag. [*laughs softly*]

MAN: [*looks out his window*] I can walk I think [*undoes seatbelt*] Which way is fastest? I don't want to get buried in the snow. That's scary, and terrible. I have to go now. I have to go.

WOMAN: [*quietly*] Please. Please sleep in my bed.

She waits for him to answer. He half-turns and looks at his feet.

MAN: I wonder if anyone is thinking about me right now.

WOMAN: No [*puts her hand back on his neck*] No you are wishing you could transform into the cigarette that is extinguished in the wetness by your feet. But you don't know the proper magical spell that would transform you. Maybe the spell is complete quiet. Yes. You are hoping the spell is complete quiet. Tag.

MAN: [*looking at his lap*] I hope the spell is complete quiet.

The woman continues to lightly scratch his neck. With her other hand she wipes some snowflakes off her lap. Both the front windows are still open and the heater is on high.

WOMAN: Do you want to sleep in my bed with me then?

MAN: [*looking at her*] If sleeping alone is bad, you should figure out how to make people like you [*pause*] Always figure out how to make people like you. Rule number one. Do that.

She ignores him. She looks out the windshield at the snow.

WOMAN: [*evenly*] It's awful to sleep alone.

MAN: I heard you [*then in unnaturally deep voice*] Fear that I will eat your body from the asshole on into complete failure.

WOMAN: [*pauses*] Would it be ok if I slept in my car, parked on your street then? Is that ok? Can I do that? At least that then.

The man puts his head in his hands.

MAN: I'm too scared to leave. But I can't let the snow bury me.

The woman turns the car off.

WOMAN: [*to no one*] I worry that all the perfect moments are accumulating in me. And that there are too many. You are in trouble when you sit down and say, 'I want to feel this, this is mine.' I think that's what's happening. All the perfect moments are trying to punish me. Punish me for thinking about hurting you. I'm sorry.

MAN: [*taking head out of hands, confused*] What?

WOMAN: [*tries not to smile*] When I was trying to park earlier—and you got out to move the shopping cart—when you did that, I had to try really hard not to press the gas down and run you over. I thought about how heavy the car would be on your body. It felt amazing thinking about how heavy the car would be on your body.

MAN: [*scratches cheek, nods*] Probably too heavy.

WOMAN: Yes. So effective [*touching his arm*] Sometimes when we are together, like right now for instance, I think about being your mom right after she had you and I am holding you and you can't tell me you don't want it anymore. Thinking about being your mother on the day of your birth and thinking about running you over with a car are the two things I love the most. You know?

The man is quiet. More snow and cold go into the car. The car is not running anymore.

WOMAN: Tag.

MAN: [*slowly*] There always has to be a loser.

The lights go out in the grocery store and the other stores in the strip mall too.

WOMAN: Tag. I think about death sometimes a lot and sometimes not at all, but when I do think about it I always think, 'Did I do everything right, is it ok?' [*as if finally admitting*] There is no bed big enough for me and there is no bed small enough for you. I know that for sure, cross my heart and hope to run you over with a car [*pause*] Tag.

They stare out the windshield at the snow. Some people exit the grocery store, say goodbye and get in their cars. Gone.

MAN: [*watching them drive away*] I'm tired in a way that will go unresolved for at least another week.

WOMAN: [*staring through the windshield*] Me too.

The wind picks up and pushes a shopping cart a little bit. The shopping cart hits a small patch of snow, stops. They both laugh and find they are holding hands.

WOMAN: You are thinking about saying "tag" but you don't want to ruin anything. You don't want to make me chase you [*pause*] Tag [*kisses his cheek*] Thank you for being here. Do you still want to walk home?

MAN: [*ignores her*] Whenever I go outside, I hope to get picked up and blown away. But it never happens. I just stand there. The wind moves around me. Yesterday I figured out that I am a small, human-shaped negative and the world is a giant space with a small human-shaped negative removed from it. And we're good for each other [*sniffs*] We're good food for each other.

WOMAN: Right.

There is loud wind. The woman wipes some snow off her cheek.

WOMAN: We will be in love until the earth grabs its chest and shrinks. Over and over again. There has to be a loser.

MAN: [*turns to the woman*] Never.

WOMAN: Oh [*reaches towards backseat*] I forgot. This is for you [*produces a package*] Happy Birthday, Arnold.

MAN: It's not my birthday.

WOMAN: Sure it is, Arnold.

MAN: [*confused*] It's not my birthday, and my name's not Arnold.

WOMAN: [*ignores*] Open it up, Arnold.

The man takes the package and undoes the wrapping paper. Inside there's a calculator.

MAN: [*looking at calculator*] Thanks.

The woman touches his arm.

WOMAN: Happy birthday, Arnold [*pointing out the window at someone crossing the parking lot*] Who's that, Arnold?

MAN: I don't know [*confused*] My name isn't Arnold [*pause*] I'm not Arnold. [*looking off to where she's pointing*]

WOMAN: [*arching her head*] Oh I think it's just a policeman [*smiling*] What do you think, Arnold?

MAN: I'm confused and scared [*holding up the gift*] Thanks for the calculator though [*reads front of the package*] "With both addition and subtraction features."

WOMAN: Look how happy that boy on the front is, doing his homework.

MAN: I see. Thank you.

WOMAN: [*toneless*] You're welcome, Arnold. You're welcome. Do you want to come home with me and play a board game or some cards with me? We don't have to go to bed. There's a wonderful board game where you get to be a little mouse. Sometimes I get angry playing the games but sometimes they make me smile and cry but I only cry once I get back to my room. Everything is leaving you once you are born. There's a wonderful board game where you get to be a little mouse. But you're lost. Will you help the little mouse out, Arnold? We can do it together and help the little mouse out. He's nice I'm sure. Do I look pretty today, Arnold?—do I? Do you want to sleep in my bed with me [*coughs*] You know, only a certain amount of people get into Heaven. They do. Every time you do something, you have to ask, 'Will this get me into Heaven? Will it?' There has to be a loser.

MAN: [*smiling*] There is too much garbage in Heaven for God to want more. There's too much garbage [*types some numbers on the calculator*] Twelve multiplied by eight is ninety-six.

More wind. Metal sounds of shopping carts drifting.

WOMAN: Can I have a hug?

MAN: [*still typing on calculator*] Can I just let you hug me or do I have to put my arms around you too?

The hug happens. The man, arms down.

MAN: That was one of my finer, more emotionally-convincing hugs I think [*looking out window*] I don't know why I got in here with you [*to himself*] This will never stop. This happens all the time.

He watches the shopping cart through his window. He is staring. The woman reaches into her pocket and takes out a switchblade. She grabs his hair with one hand and with the other hand she cuts his neck open, sawing deep.

MAN: [*bleeding into lap, where both his hands are palms up*] Why did I get in the car?

He looks at the clock.

WOMAN: [*wiping knife off on her shirt*] You are calculating the hours remaining before you will get tired and go to bed.

The man turns from the clock to her.

WOMAN: [*puts knife up to his face*] And you regret even calculating because you know any answer will upset you. Tag.

They wait to be buried in snow.

THE BASTARDS [THEY MAKE PEACE WITH MOTHER EARTH]

Daytime. Three men drive down a road that threads a forest preserve. The man in the passenger's seat is loading a shotgun. His neck is cut deep, bleeding pumps he sighs out in slow intervals onto his lap. He is very weak. The windows are all open.

THE DRIVER: [*scratching sideburn*] I am thinking something.

THE MAN FROM THE BACKSEAT: [*rocking back and forth*] Hold on, stop talking. I can't remember what my mom looks like [*panicked*] It's difficult to do for some reason and I'm getting scared [*stops rocking*] I keep trying to remember. I can't do it. It's impossible [*then louder*] It's impossible.

The man with the slit-throat pumps a cartridge into place. He looks at his hands. They are pale. He wheezes something that he thinks probably isn't a word but should be.

THE MAN WITH THE SLIT-THROAT: [*sitting up weakly, keeping chin down*] God bless America. I really mean that.

THE MAN FROM THE BACKSEAT: [*composed*] Ok, I remembered what she looks like [*to the driver*] I believe you were thinking something. Sorry I interrupted like that. It helped though. Fuck, that was weird. What were you thinking? Come on. Tell us.

THE MAN WITH THE SLIT-THROAT: [*quietly*] Yeah. Tell us.

THE DRIVER: Yeah, can I say it now? After I think things, I have to say them.

The man with the slit-throat positions the gun in his mouth. He secures it with his legs. Then he flicks fuzz off his pants.

THE DRIVER: [*looking at the man with the slit-throat*] Hey, you'll ruin your appetite for dinner mister [*stops*] I don't know why I said that [*looking into the rearview mirror*] Anyway, what I was thinking before was that Santa Claus is probably the invention of a pedophile [*looking forward again*] Think about it. It's a perfect way to keep a kid quiet about breaking into his or her room and then assaulting them. Also, the whole milk and cookies thing is genius right—I'm always hungry after a sexual assault [*pauses*] and for one.

They all laugh.

THE MAN FROM THE BACKSEAT: [*rubs chin*] This explains why I always got bruised wrists for Christmas.

The man with the slit-throat mumbles something. The gun in his mouth holds him up, neck open in wet flaps. Blood pumps onto his limp hands, both lapped.

THE DRIVER: Hey [*pauses*] Quit being rude [*laughing*]

They all laugh. The man with the slit-throat takes the gun out of his mouth. He wipes his mouth. Then he looks out the window, chin down to clamp the slit-throat together. He is weak.

THE MAN WITH THE SLIT-THROAT: [*quietly*] Sorry. I was saying that that explains why I always got a face scraped up by beard hair and a neck covered in bite marks.

THE DRIVER: Yes, and that explains why I always got nothing because I was an unattractive child.

THE MAN FROM THE BACKSEAT: I got my mom a sore neck for Christmas last year but it was the wrong size. I don't respect anyone else's life. That is my main problem. That and never really knowing whether or not other people like me, or if I like them. I am very angry. Believe that I am very angry [*looks out window*] There is no one thing that is important. And I am very angry.

They drive. Climbing a slight hill, the sun blinks in rapid clips, trees blacking out strobes. All three squint against the machine-gunning of the sun.

THE DRIVER: [*squinting through the window*] I was also thinking something else, you know, before you interrupted me [*bites nails*] I was thinking the sky is the big breath that everyone ever made has breathed. Does that make sense to anyone else right now?

The man with the slit-throat puts the gun back into his mouth and pushes it in deep. He pulls the trigger and his head explodes, flapping open with wet heat. The other two grimace from ringing ears, and they taste burn in their mouths.

THE DRIVER: [*takes a few looks at the exploded head*] His head looks like orange peels.

THE MAN FROM THE BACKSEAT: Huh? [*blinking to restrain watering eyes, hands over ears*] My fucking ears are bleeding. I can't hear you.

THE DRIVER: [*eyes in rearview*] I was just saying his head looks like orange peels—that's how I would describe it.

THE MAN FROM THE BACKSEAT: [*examines exploded head*] Yes, in one sense, but not in terms of the smell. I don't like oranges—they're too much work to peel. It's not worth it [*insistent*] I hate when you have to do things to make other things happen. Like, for instance, as stated, peeling an orange.

THE DRIVER: [*sniffs*] Looks like he had an easy time.

They both laugh and the driver taps the steering wheel.

THE DRIVER: [*to himself*] I do really like oranges though.

THE MAN FROM THE BACKSEAT: [*not listening, still laughing lightly*] Shit. You were always the funny one. How do you come up with that stuff? Seriously.

THE DRIVER: [*adjusts himself in seat, excited*] I don't know man, it just comes to me. I swear. I swear it's just out of nowhere. I remember this one time I was at the supermarket and I was walking down the aisle and I almost ran into this lady—so we kept sidestepping in the same direction. Want to know what I said? Do you want to know?

THE MAN FROM THE BACKSEAT: [*wiping some blood off his face onto the car seat*] You know I do, big-guy.

The driver pushes the body in the passenger seat, so the wound hangs out the window. The wound sprays the backseat through the open windows.

THE DRIVER: Well [*eyes and eyebrows in the rearview*] I said, "May I have this dance?" And I offered my hands like I really was going to dance with her [*his eyebrows curl*] She was all confused!

They both laugh. The driver removes blood from his ears using his smallest finger.

THE MAN FROM THE BACKSEAT: Super funny. You are definitely the funniest person I know. Way funnier than the deer bones I keep underneath my bed. They don't ever say anything funny. Not like you man.

THE DRIVER: [*coughs into hand, then absently toned*] Funny times a million bajillion [*turns*] Hey, did the stuff inside his head get on you at all?

THE MAN FROM THE BACKSEAT: A little bit yeah. Wait, what's it called again?

THE DRIVER: [*quickly*] It's called thoughts.

THE MAN FROM THE BACKSEAT: [*smallest finger shoveling blood from ear*] No. I think it's called blood. Blood. Does that sound right?

THE DRIVER: Not sure [*rolls down window further*] I forget words all the time. I understand myself through what words I still remember and which ones I can't remember [*pause*] So none of his—blood—got on you then?

THE MAN FROM THE BACKSEAT: I feel like I should've had a poncho on, like I was at a Gallagher performance.

THE DRIVER: [*excited*] I remember Gallagher. Do you think he's still alive? It's hard to decide.

THE MAN FROM THE BACKSEAT: For some reason I imagine that he is overdosing on the bathroom floor at a gas station. Or maybe he's just in a gas station bathroom, combing the hair around his ears. And he isn't smiling. He can never figure out how to style the hair around his ears. There is very little of the hair around his ears but he tries so hard to make it look nice.

THE DRIVER: [*ignores*] You never know. You can be anything you want when you grow up.

The man in the backseat puts his hand into the peeled head and then presses his hand over the driver's face. The driver laughs. They pass a road sign with a message spraypainted over it that says: "Stay Home"

THE DRIVER: Thank you. Thank you for the handprint on my face. I guarantee you have improved the value of my body.

THE MAN FROM THE BACKSEAT: [*head in front of car, arms on each headrest*] You know, this whole thing settles a bet I had with someone. We were arguing about what's actually in your head. He bet me that inside a human head there are gummy bears and thumbtacks. He was pretty insistent. But now I know he was wrong. Now I know there is, blood. And no soul [*claps*] We've figured out a lot today. I always feel better going to sleep if I know I figured something out during the day [*taps headrests*] This is good.

THE DRIVER: [*puts left forearm through open window*] Well, look around do you see any gummy bears or thumbtacks?

The man in the backseat looks around. He checks his pockets and the floor and leans forward over the dead body and checks the glovebox. He takes out a small object.

THE MAN FROM THE BACKSEAT: There's a thumbtack in the glovebox but maybe that was there already? It seems hard to believe that he shot the insides of his head, like, into the glovebox. That would be too mysterious. I don't think that can even happen. I'd be scared out of my mind.

THE DRIVER: Oh me too [*pause*] Hey can you sit back down and put your seatbelt on? I'm getting nervous. But yes, that thumbtack was in there already. I was tacking up some of my old gradeschool math exams the other day. My self-esteem has been low lately [*eyes in rearview*] I become randomly disappointed in myself and then I look at the grades on the math exams and the stickers with the smiling faces. It makes me feel better.

THE MAN FROM THE BACKSEAT: [*scared*] Hold on, I forgot what my mom looks like again [*sits back*] I'm upset that my head is the only place that most of the world exists. I could just make up what she looks like but then she'll be different every time. She'll be a stranger every time. [*rocking back and forth*]

THE DRIVER: [*reaches over to the passenger seat*] It is mean of you to keep your mom locked up inside your head. You should let her out.

The driver grabs the bloody shotgun from between the dead person's legs and offers it to the man in the backseat, smiles.

THE MAN FROM THE BACKSEAT: Nice try, Mr. Joker.

They laugh.

THE DRIVER: [*still laughing, smiling*] You can't blame me for trying [*quickly not smiling*] To be honest, I just didn't want to have to give you a ride home.

They pull over and take the man with the exploded head out of the car and throw him into a ditch along the forest preserve. The driver kicks some leaves over the ripped head.

THE DRIVER: [*pointing*] Look, an ostrich.

THE MAN FROM THE BACKSEAT: [*blowing into cupped hands*] You are the silliest person ever [*looks up at forest*] Wait, something is wrong. I am still very angry. Can't stop feeling angry. Something is wrong [*back and forth, looks from dead body to forest*] I'm so angry.

They both look at the forest. The trees shake, building slow into volume, then stop in equally slow gradation. Wind.

THE DRIVER: [*toneless*] Something is wrong.

Neither says anything for a while.

THE MAN FROM THE BACKSEAT: Can we stop by the library on the way home? I have to drop off a book. I owe forty-five cents and I don't want the women at the library to question my responsibility. I've been pretty good about establishing myself as a reliable person over there. I don't want all that squandered so quickly. Don't let forty-five cents separate me from seeming responsible to older women.

THE DRIVER: Alright.

They get back in the car. They drive. The handprint cools on the driver's face and he rubs it off into little crumbs that he throws down by his feet, into the brush of the floormat. Taking a curve, the passing trees and the wind create a chopping sound through the window. They listen to the chopping sound and stare out the windshield. Paralyzed, staring blinkless.

THE DRIVER: [*quietly*] This is the most successful day ever and I hope it never ends. Hey, you can sit in the front seat if you want [*tapping seat*] I feel lonely up here all by myself.

THE MAN FROM THE BACKSEAT: [*looks at the seat, then the driver*] I don't want to sit in that seat, there's, blood, all over it. And I just bought these pants.

THE DRIVER: [*turns head slightly*] Yeah those are really nice. I was going to say something but I thought you might feel weird about me confessing to looking at your legs and butt or whatever. Some guys are like that.

THE MAN FROM THE BACKSEAT: Oh no. Not me. Attention from other humans is the only way to remember that I am alive. It is also the only way to hate being alive. Weird. I hope my grave is big enough to have people over.

THE DRIVER: Yeah? How many people? That sounds like fun.

THE MAN FROM THE BACKSEAT: Everyone that ever existed and does exist.

They're quiet for a while. They pass long curves of the forest preserve. There is no one out, but there is garbage on the forest floor and the road. The loud chopping sound continues through the window and when they climb a hill it synchs with the sun—in strobes—light and noise at the same time repeating. They stare silently. Rounding a tighter curve, a deer jumps out. The car collides with the deer. The deer's body explodes, cracking the windshield fully. And it slides off the car when the car breaks, landing on the stick and leaf covered road. The chopping sound has ended. The deer convulses on the ground. It kneels on its front two legs, trying to stand. Blood shines both nose and face and it falls to its knees again—front leg broken horribly, front leg sideways and ashed with blacktop along the break.

THE DRIVER: [*staring through the windshield with blood on his face*] Some cars are made of steel and some are made of fur and bones. The ones that are made of steel will always win. Yeah.

THE MAN FROM THE BACKSEAT: Definitely. I feel good when I watch something die. It makes me feel powerful. I guess I am a little hurt when I see it, but also very good. Too good. I'm not angry now anymore. I am a car made of steel and the earth only makes things out of fur and bone. And I made myself. Being a human is better than being the earth I think. I'm not even angry any more. I can't remember what anger looks like. It is not in my head now anymore.

THE DRIVER: [*wipes some blood off his face*] Faces are the worst of human possessions.

THE MAN FROM THE BACKSEAT: Yes but yours is so pretty [*puts hand on the driver's shoulder*] It was made after the earth got a manicure.

The driver gives a thumbs-up sign into the rearview mirror.

THE DRIVER: Let's check on our friend.

THE MAN FROM THE BACKSEAT: [*undoing seatbelt*] Friends make the world go round.

They get out of the car and look at the deer. The deer lies angled, its jaw missing and its front leg held only by skin. When the deer moves its broken leg only the top half moves, the other half remains on the road, heavy. And the two men watch the trees reflect off its open black eyes.

THE DRIVER: Much like your mother being in your mind, the trees are now only in the eyes of this dying animal. Very interesting. What does that mean? I am fucking confused about everything right now. Hold on. Wait—I'm good now, nevermind. I don't care.

THE MAN FROM THE BACKSEAT: [*turns to the driver*] Should we cut its eyes open and make the trees free? Is that what you are saying? They need to be free. I love the earth. It is our mother [*touches head, confused*] Wait that means the world is in my mind [*panicked*] I will take care of the earth by thinking about it. Should we cut the deer's eyes open and free the forest? I don't know what to do now. I'm confused about everything now. I'm angry. Let's cut the eyes open.

THE DRIVER: [*still eyeing deer pile*] No, let's just watch it die. No one thing that is alive is important. Let's just leave it alone. We'll watch.

THE MAN FROM THE BACKSEAT: You read my mind.

They look at the bloody road. They kick small stones, some sticking to the deer's nose. The deer is quiet.

THE MAN FROM THE BACKSEAT: [*staring at deer*] Hey, would you mind if I use that 'may I have this dance?' line sometime?

THE DRIVER: If you properly cite it, then yes.

Silence. They stare up, above the forest. The deer wheezes. Keeps wheezing. They hear the muscles struggling in its throat but they do not look. Instead they stare up. There is no one out but there is garbage everywhere. Harsh clacks of coughing from the deer's throat muscles. Then nothing. Both men laugh.

THE DRIVER: Well? Shall we?

They carry the deer into the forest and bring it to the nearest loop of a stream.

THE MAN FROM THE BACKSEAT: [*putting hand on tree, stepping over shallow area of stream*] If my shoes get wet I am going to lie down and not get up.

THE DRIVER: Then your back would be wet too.

THE MAN FROM THE BACKSEAT: [*sneezes*] It wouldn't matter at that point.

THE DRIVER: There is nothing to be upset about without being selfish [*setting his end of deer down*] If your shoes get wet and you decide to lie down, I won't tell anyone where you are. Alright?

THE MAN FROM THE BACKSEAT: [*kneeling by the deer with the driver*] I would be scared lying down all by myself [*puts hand into the area where the deer's jaw was*]

THE DRIVER: [*reaching in too*] The only way to feel comfortable on earth is to constantly try to prove to others that you are worthwhile. Otherwise there is no excuse for you to be here. No single thing is important.

They pull down on the wound and rip the body open. The man from the backseat works on taking the bones out while the driver washes them in the stream. In quiet they wash. When finished, they stack the bones by the stream and walk off, back towards the car.

THE DRIVER: When I breathe, my breath looks like fog. The breath goes into the fog and it becomes the sky. I don't want to donate to the sky. I want everything to be mine and only mine. The bigger breath is above the sky.

He blows out and they both watch.

THE MAN FROM THE BACKSEAT: Thanks for spending time with me today. Usually on the weekends I lie in bed for a long time after I wake up. And I watch the fibers floating in the air. I can see them when the sun comes into the window. I name them and think about their lives. I wonder if they ever land. Sometimes I try to watch one land. It's impossible to see though. I don't know, thanks for spending time with me. I don't love you or anything, but I'm grateful. You make me smile.

THE DRIVER: Saying 'I love you' is the stupidest thing ever. It means nothing.

THE MAN FROM THE BACKSEAT: I agree. It is painful to be visible.

They begin walking back. A raccoon climbs a short tree trunk across from them, huge black eyes pointed their way. The raccoon runs away, into a rotten tree. They stand still.

THE DRIVER: I see raccoons every night when I go for walks. They are always out. They always run away from me. I want to touch them. But they will never let me touch them [*clears throat*] they always run away. I don't believe in souls. I believe in bones. And I believe that the earth is the biggest garbage dump there is. Some of the garbage can still move and some can't move anymore. But there is no difference.

THE MAN FROM THE BACKSEAT: [*drumming on thighs*] The garbage that can't move teaches the garbage that still moves.

They see another raccoon. The driver walks slowly towards the raccoon. It runs away. They return to the car, walking slow and tapping their hands against the trees. The bloodstain on the street is already less bright, and a tire track extends through it, into the invisible distance.

THE DRIVER: The earth makes shitty merchandise. A car of steel will always kill a car of fur and bone. And a hand will always kill a smaller hand.

THE MAN FROM THE BACKSEAT: And a knife will always kill a hand.

THE DRIVER: And a gun will always kill a knife.

THE MAN FROM THE BACKSEAT: And a bomb will always kill a gun.

THE DRIVER: And a drop of water will always kill a bomb.

THE MAN FROM THE BACKSEAT: And the sun will kill the water.

THE DRIVER: And time will kill the sun.

THE MAN FROM THE BACKSEAT: And a human will always kill time.

THE DRIVER: And time will always kill a human.

THE MAN FROM THE BACKSEAT: And complete disregard will kill a human.

THE DRIVER: And a car made of steel will always kill a car made of fur and bone.

THE MAN FROM THE BACKSEAT: And we will always smile unless we forget to clean our teeth [*quiet, looking at bloodstain, then facing the driver*] Uh [*breathes heavily*] I am feeling something like a bubble in my stomach [*rocks back and forth*] Fuck I might cry. My insides are yawning. I might cry. What is happening right now? This is bad [*louder*] Help me through this [*then quiet*] I'm so angry. The deer is in my head now, with my mom. And this bloodstain. They don't all like each other. Everything is upsetting me [*tearing-up*] shit, now my face is sinking. There's water coming out of me. Please don't tell anyone about this. It feels good but it feels bad to let you see it [*louder*] I'm angry you are looking at me.

THE DRIVER: [*hand on other man's shoulder*] Don't worry. Your mom will pet the deer and love it. And they will sit on the bloodstain. Everything will be fine. Don't be upset, let your face sink. Sinking and drowning are peaceful ways to die. There are as many ways to die as there are people. Get it? How it happens makes you who you are. It is happening to me now but I'm not letting it show [*soft tone*] If your face drowns, you will find peace. And I won't tell anyone. Your mom will be nice to the deer and they will figure out life together, sitting on the bloodstain. Be fine now.

THE MAN FROM THE BACKSEAT: [*staring at the bloodstain*] No I don't want them in there together. That's my mom. She must be held above all other things. When I think about my mom, I try to immediately think of me too so we can be together. But it is impossible to think about myself. [*breathes heavily, teary-eyed*]

He runs to the car and grabs the gun from the floormat. He shoots himself in the mouth and falls to the road, bleeding from what is now a wedge between his shoulders, in a long sprawl that joins the deer's. Bloodstain made bright again. The driver stands in it.

THE DRIVER: I kind of feel like jumping up and down and splashing and having fun. But my dad already taught me never to have fun.

He stands in the stain and looks up above the forest.

THE DRIVER: I will always be the last one standing. The earth makes weak products, but didn't make me. The earth makes shitty merchandise. This is a terrarium and the heatlamp is the sky's smile and everyone wants to touch it. I am fine with being alone.

He gets in the car and puts his seatbelt on. Drives away. He reaches to the passenger seat, but the gun is gone.

THE DRIVER: [*looking at the bloodstained seat*] God bless this mess.

He drives through the rest of the forest and comes to an intersection. There, he sees other cars. The other cars confuse him. He begins to cry. He sits in his car, crying.

THE DRIVER: The face drowns. This will be peaceful.

There is a knock in the back of the car. Then more knocking. The driver wipes his face and gets out of the car. He opens the trunk and he lets out a person wearing an ankle length sheet with eyeholes removed. The person in the sheet runs away, appearing to float. Then a car hits the person, and the person lies still.

THE POLICEMAN IS A FORM OF PUNISHMENT

The livingroom of a single story house. A boyfriend and a girlfriend stand in the livingroom, kneedeep in dust. And they look out the room's large window into the front yard area. Neither the boyfriend or the girlfriend have eaten in years. Starved very thin, they are looking out the window at the lawn. It's fall, and there are leaves and sticks all over the ground. Standing on the front lawn there is a policeman, holding a rifle. He is on the lawn looking back at them through the window, pointing the rifle at them. Clouds and sun on projectors above the single story house.

BOYFRIEND: [*not looking at girlfriend*] He's still there.

The girlfriend balances herself with a hand on his shoulder while she scratches her shin with the toes on her other foot.

GIRLFRIEND: He will be with us forever [*resigned*] And I don't even know the color of his eyes.

BOYFRIEND: [*slow blinking*] I thought he would be gone for some reason. But I think he's going to stay. He is not getting thinner either. We're getting thinner. We are the ones who are getting thinner.

GIRLFRIEND: Even though I am terrified that he will come into our house and kill me, or yikes [*hand to mouth, mocking*] kill you first and make me watch [*looks at him*] I'm kind of relieved that now the lawn won't float away, because he is standing on it. Yes he is doing a good job. If you think about it like that, he's doing a great job.

The boyfriend continues staring out the window at the policeman. He pinches his girlfriend's neck and she winces, crying.

BOYFRIEND: Yes I am sometimes grateful to the ceiling because it won't allow me to float away. I am getting thinner. We are the ones getting thinner.

GIRLFRIEND: [*cries a few drops into the dust*] I can't tell if it is worse to have eyes or not have them.

The boyfriend does not look away from the window.

BOYFRIEND: [*flatly*] Can you tell that I am getting thinner? Do you feel sick looking at me? I haven't eaten in so long I see neon colored particles raining on me from the ceiling and when it's time to float I guess I will stand still. I will act like I agree.

GIRLFRIEND: [*wipes eyes*] You are getting sick and very thin and I can tell that you are a weak, weak motherfucker [*through snot and hiccups*] If we hold each other we won't float away [*clears her throat, sniffs*] He's still standing there.

BOYFRIEND: He will always be with us. He will never float away. He'll hold the lawn in place. Which is good because we can't afford another lawn unless dust becomes money.

GIRLFRIEND: And because we stopped counting, we don't know the date.

They stand in the livingroom and the rifle stares back. The sun and clouds on the projectors darken. It gets dark and the three of them stare at each other even though they can't see. They stand through the night, and say nothing. Next day, the same situation. They continue to thin.

BOYFRIEND: [*having difficulty talking*] I can't tell if he is still alive or not. It seems hard to tell. Not sure I can see at all anymore. Every dead body is a tumor in this earth. Is that how you see things? Can we talk?

GIRLFRIEND: [*putting her thin hair behind her ear*] He's still standing. Standing means still alive. He is still with us [*looks directly at boyfriend*] You are still standing too—but that's my decision [*points at own chest*] I am letting that happen. Remember that, you weak motherfucker. You are a weak motherfucker. If I lie down you would never be able to pick me up. You were born to grow thin enough to float. Get ready. Because I'm not coming with. You're going alone.

The clouds and the sun on the projector above go black-lighted.

BOYFRIEND: Up until now, I always thought that dying was something that happened to everyone else, but it didn't necessarily have to happen to me. Is that strange? I mean, I've ruined my day so many times it happens without me noticing now. Is that strange? I don't want to leave the house because I am concerned about the policeman. Very concerned. But, also, almost ready to die.

The boyfriend starts crying. He kneels in the dust. He is hideous, cartoonish. And the girlfriend eats some dust off the ground, let's a few handfuls fall to boyfriend's head.

GIRLFRIEND: [*dust hanging from mouth*] Whenever I see another human crying, I feel angry. That's my first reaction [*pauses, then in tone of warning*] The more you cry the thinner you will be. And there are times I know I am being petty and terrible and other times I don't care. Right now [*wiping dust off mouth*] I don't care. When I see another human crying, I feel angry.

BOYFRIEND: Then please don't look at me [*wiping face with forearm*] Please don't.

GIRLFRIEND: I try not to [*scoops more dust, drops it on the boyfriend's head*] I can't even keep my balance when I see your face. Just, overcome with anger. I kind of itch. Does that make sense?

BOYFRIEND: [*staring out the window, trying to blink off dust*] You are a weak motherfucker.

The girlfriend laughs and cleans off her boyfriend's face with her hands. She laughs at him.

GIRLFRIEND: Alright do you want me to ask him to go away? I will do that for you. Maybe if I just ask him, he'll leave [*then to herself*] I need to know the color of his eyes. I need to see them. Just that.

BOYFRIEND: [*nods his head, still crying*] Jesus Christ [*he burps and some bile sours his mouth*] We can't leave the house. I'm too scared.

GIRLFRIEND: Do you want me to ask him to leave? Say please and I'll do it. You're getting so thin it is almost time for you to rise into the air. Should I ask him to leave?

BOYFRIEND: Please.

They kiss, the boyfriend still kneeling. She drops some dust on his head and laughs. They are together.

GIRLFRIEND: Your mouth tastes horrible.

BOYFRIEND: [*looking down*] I know. It's because I am hungry. Don't kiss me if it tastes bad then. You have to have an appetite for a kiss, just like food and sleep and other things, friends maybe too.

GIRLFRIEND: [*smiles and pinches his sick face*] I always have an appetite for a kiss.

BOYFRIEND: Please ask him to leave [*pause*] I don't think I have ever come like I want to. Like I really want to [*balls fists and puts them over his eyes*] Please go tell him to leave [*apologetically*] I just want to watch tv with you in bed. I want to act like the tv is a third person with us. Ask him to leave so I can come like I really want to. Alright?

The clouds on the projector again go bright. And the girlfriend drops a last handful of dust on the boyfriend's head then looks at him with contempt. She walks outside and stands in front of the policeman. The policeman is trembling. He rubs his face repeatedly with his shoulder—still aiming the rifle at the house.

GIRLFRIEND: [*hand over eyes, squinting*] Why are you with us?

POLICEMAN: [*wiping face*] I don't know where I am. I just don't [*presenting the rifle to her*] Here, please take this. I can barely stand holding it. I don't know where I am. The middle of the earth is pulling me down, please take this [*hands rifle over, wipes his face and panics*] The fucking sand. It's coming out of my face. I can't get it off. I wish I had eighteen hands so I could brush the sand off. If I had eighteen hands I would split the hands and the nerves would multiply and then I would have three hundred minus forty hands and then I could brush the sand off. I need to scrape the inside of my skin off. That's where it comes from I think. I haven't been hard in months. I am getting buried. And the middle of the earth is the criminal that's stealing me.

GIRLFRIEND: [*inspects rifle idly*] When you are fully buried I will walk over the mound just to see what the other side looks like. The middle of the earth will pull you very deep and then smooth out the bump that is you on the world's carpet.

POLICEMAN: [*slapping at his face*] I can't get it off my fucking face.

And I can't push it back in. I think I am going to let it bury me—that will be quicker, yeah I'll do that, yes ok [*stops, notices rifle is pointed at his face*] There is nothing in there. In your hands you hold a negated weapon-thing, you hold nothing. There is nothing inside.

GIRLFRIEND: [*lowering the rifle*] Oh [*laughs, embarrassed*] no I was just going to help you with the sand on your face. Don't you want help? I can get it off for you.

POLICEMAN: No. I mean there are only spiders in there. The gun is filled with spiders. Yesterday I was going to point it at the sky and shoot an escape route but then I remembered there is nothing in there. Just spiders.

The policeman slaps at his face and rubs it. He is irritated. The girlfriend undoes the bolt and little orange spiders fall out. She stands back to let the spiders fall to her feet. Then she steps on them a few times to make sure they are all dead.

POLICEMAN: [*watching*] I don't blame you. They are killers [*wiping his face*] But they won't kill me. Nothing kills me. No. Nothing helps me [*eyes narrow*] I want to kill your boyfriend. I think I would forget about the sand for a second if I could kill your weakling boyfriend. I see him staring at me. I will not let him leave. After I shoot the escape route I seal it with happy tears. I will never get the sand off my face but I will escape. With your boyfriend dead—with your boyfriend's blood all over my face to cool off—I escape.

The girlfriend clicks the bolt back into position. More spiders fall out. She steps on them. And the clouds and the sun on the projector go black-lighted. All things are open.

POLICEMAN: The spiders will come back. The spiders are like the sand. The spiders and the sand are the same thing I guess. The sand has little legs. No one can help me get it off. I feel weak [*rakes face with fingers*] I need to lie down. You can't count sand. You can only feel it. I murdered these other people once. The last house I was guarding. The only people I have told are you and the grassblades at my feet, at night. So the last house I guarded, I knocked on the door and they let me in. I didn't feel ok. I was standing there lying to both of them about something, because I just wanted to see them up close. That's when I heard the refrigerator start to drone. It got really loud.

I couldn't stand it. It hurt my head. I stared at the refrigerator. The people were talking to me. They were so thin. I couldn't hear them. And I got confused. Then the woman started to run and her husband grabbed me. I realized I had my gun in my hands and I had shot the man in the thigh. He was bleeding a lot, from a huge mess of splayed tissue. His wife tried to go upstairs—but she didn't step two feet away [*raises two fingers*] —not two feet, before I nailed her. I nailed her. I don't even think I thought, I just shot. I shot her right in the fucking waist. Pretty much cut her in half. I mean I did cut her in half. And she let out the sickest moan, then kind of withered up. A human looks strange when there is only half of it. But I loved it. I just watched. I had to watch it. It was the nicest piece of art I ever made. I had to push her husband, or whatever he was, into the wall. He was still attacking me. I maced him and kicked his face until he was quiet. The refrigerator droned loudly. I felt sand all over my face. It stuck to me. I kept itching and yelling to compete with the droning refrigerator. The looks on both their faces when they died were horrible, but I felt powerful for having seen them. The looks on their faces were like they were about to ask a question [*thumb into chest*] I'm a role model. I'm a great human. I don't think I've ever done anything wrong. I don't have any regard for other human life. When I searched their house, I found a nailgun. I spent the rest of the night shooting nails into the man's stomach. It's ok though—he didn't feel it [*breathes in, then out heavily*] The people I killed and the sand are the same thing. The people I killed are the sand. The sun will not set tonight.

Above them, the clouds and the sun return to brightness. And the girlfriend puts the rifle over her shoulder. She squints, blocking the light with her hands.

GIRLFRIEND: How do you feel?

POLICEMAN: [*looking beyond her, to the boyfriend*] I don't know what's happening. I feel this way all the time. I don't know what's happening. I know that it is happening. There is no doubt that it is happening [*breathes out heavily*] Be nice to me please. The sun will not set tonight.

The policeman wipes his face repeatedly. He is irritated. And he directs some of the sand into the gun's barrel. Then he lies down and hugs the girlfriend's feet. He looks up, hugging her feet tight and squinting into the air.

GIRLFRIEND: You are a weak motherfucker [*motions the sign of the cross in front of the policeman*] There you go. You're good now. You're still one of the angels. You're still a weak motherfucker. You can be forgiven for things by not remembering them. You silly willy.

She puts the rifle in the policeman's mouth and pushes it in deep. The policeman gags. He blinks water out of his eyes and tries to say something. He tries to indicate that the gun is not loaded. But he gives up, and instead smiles and points. Drool falls out his smile. He makes a gun motion with his thumb and forefinger. The girlfriend shoots the policeman and he sleeps on a pile of his own maroon-colored slop. Burn marks rim his mouth and smoke leaves a hole in his head. But he is still himself. The smoke rises and the girlfriend gets on her hands and knees and inhales the smoke. She inhales the smoke from the shattered head and then returns to the house, stands next to her boyfriend. She puts her arm around his shoulder and blows the smoke in his face. They look out the window together. The clouds and sun on the projectors above again go black-lighted.

BOYFRIEND: [*looking at the policeman*] His shadow is the same shape as his body [*tone suggesting obviousness*] Except where the sun comes in through the head I mean.

The girlfriend undoes the bolt on the rifle and more spiders fall out. Then she pokes her boyfriend's head with the hot rifletip.

GIRLFRIEND: You are a weak motherfucker.

The boyfriend laughs. The girlfriend laughs and puts the rifle over her shoulder. They hug, girlfriend facing the window, boyfriend other way. They both feel around on each other's bodies and determine the thinness. They are gentle while they feel.

BOYFRIEND: [*looking over girlfriend's shoulder, at the dust*] Everything is made-up.

GIRLFRIEND: [watching *the policeman stand up, stare back*] I agree.

It gets darker but the sun is still out.

BE NICE TO EVERYONE [VERSION 4]

A woman lets a man into her apartment. He sits at the table in her kitchen. On the table there's a withered plant. The plant has areas of brown on its leaves.

MAN: [*flicking some leaves off*] Almost there.

The woman shuts and locks the door then comes into the kitchen.

WOMAN: What?

MAN: [*folding his hands and looking up to her*] Did you get your period yet?

They look at each other quietly. They forget every word that ever existed, even "forget."

THE PEDOPHILE [AND HIS KINDNESS]

A small clearing in a forest preserve at the bottom of a slope. Standing in the clearing there's a pedophile with his arm against a tree. The tree is filled with skeletons. A nest of them. The pedophile wears an old gray sweatsuit. His head is shaven in random patches and there are scabs all over his head and face, covered in dry dirt. He is looking up at the skeletons when a small boy comes tripping down the slope, into the clearing. The boy wears a winter coat, and carries a rake. He stands, breathing and watching his breath.

THE BOY: Hi [*hands rake over*] Here. Here you go [*relieved, breathing heavily*] I've been thinking about outerspace all day. I'm worried about it falling over the whole planet. I'm worried about it being very cold, not all warm and nice like my real blanket [*breathes heavily*]

The pedophile takes the rake without turning. With his other hand he reaches into his pocket and takes out a mask made from a garbagebag, puts it over his head.

THE PEDOPHILE: [*still looking up*] Every year this happens [*steam from mask*] When it stops, I think it is done. When it continues I remember it will never be done.

The boy looks up and breathes. Watches his breath. He licks sweat off his lip. The pedophile lifts the rake up into the bare branches of the tree and knocks down a skeleton. When the skeleton hits the ground, its skull powders on a rock and reveals a replica underneath—a replica made of blue glass. The pedophile holds the blue glass skull in his arms like a baby and looks at it.

THE PEDOPHILE: Every year, the same thing happens. They always come. I don't think things will ever be different [*breathes*] I'm never going to die [*then brightening*] But, I mean, there's nothing you can do right? They are going to come either way.

THE BOY: I don't know what you're talking about. I'm the one who will never die.

The boy runs back up the hill, out of the clearing. The pedophile sets the blue glass skull on the ground and breaks it with the rake.

THE PEDOPHILE: They are still with me.

[*Next Day.*]

The boy enters the clearing, another rake in hand. The pedophile stands by the tree, one hand on his chin and one hand on his hip. He takes the rake, knocks down another skeleton. The skeleton falls right by the boy's feet.

THE PEDOPHILE: [*taking the rake prongs down from the branches*] I like when they break, it makes me feel intense pressure in my groin.

THE BOY: Sorta. It only broke—right there [*pointing*]

He wipes snot off his face with his hand. Then he kicks the skeleton and it collapses.

THE BOY: [*laughing*] Now it's broken. Now it is definitely all broken.

He throws his hands into the air and screams and jumps and falls to the ground, laughing. He kicks and his boots thud against the ground, ground stiff with ice. The pedophile's throat backs up with semen. And he tries to swallow it all before he chokes and cries, but he can't. He stares, entranced by the thudding of the boots on the ground.

THE PEDOPHILE: [*to himself*] Maybe that's what his skull would sound like, repeatedly pounded with the handle-end of the rake. I want to know [*gags more*] Over and over. It feels better each time.

The boy squirms, and the pedophile watches, putting his sleeve into his mouth to soak what's spilling. His sleeve is already hard, and it horrifies him going into his mouth. The hard sleeve scratches the roof of his mouth and makes him gag violently.

THE PEDOPHILE: This feels horrible [*coughs more semen*] Everything is so terrible [*he sees the boy squirming and laughing*] You are the silliest person I know. And I like you.

Semen hangs from his mouth and hand. It hits the ground. His mouth is rimmed with it.

THE PEDOPHILE: I like you. I like you and I like when you are here. We have fun. I like each of your little legs. They are so small. They are little flutes. Can I play one? Can I try one?

He goes to tickle the boy as the boy gets up. The boy dodges him and laughs.

THE BOY: My legs are not flutes.

THE PEDOPHILE: Let me play one. I will make it sound nice. I can hold your leg and make it a flute and no one would know. I'll play a song that makes you go blind.

The pedophile takes off his garbagebag mask and the muscles in his face loosen and his face sags over his eyes and mouth.

THE PEDOPHILE: Give me your little flute, you slut bitch. Give it to me. Why don't you want to kiss me? I think you want to kiss me. Right? Do you want to kiss me? [*drooling semen over shirt*] Fucking little faggot. Kiss me. Right? Huh? Give me a kiss.

THE BOY: [*looking up at the tree*] You are not right.

He runs back up the hill. The pedophile looks at the tree, and the skeletons.

THE PEDOPHILE: [*after long breath*] If I don't remove them, I will have no place to sleep. If I don't remove them they will pile until they poke a hole in outerspace and subject the world to the bigger sun on the other side. The one that is too powerful. If I don't remove them, I will never have privacy.

The pedophile puts the garbagebag mask on.

THE PEDOPHILE: I should at least pull down a few more.

He throws sticks at the skeletons. The boy has taken the rake. And the pedophile sits down, tired.

[*Next Day.*]

The boy doesn't come. The pedophile stays at the bottom of the hill and looks at all the skeletons piling up in the bare branches of the tree. They are threaded and piled thickly. More now.

THE PEDOPHILE: I am too tired for anything.

He looks at some broken sticks on the ground and slouches, breathing evenly to keep from crying.

THE PEDOPHILE: My terrible mind is my periscope, and I need it to see islands.

He kneels and leans his face against the tree.

[*Next Day.*]

The boy remains absent. The pedophile looks at the branches of the tree, piling up the skeletons, one hand on his chin and one hand on his hip. Even more now.

THE PEDOPHILE: They are still with me. Is it good that this happens? It is unbearable sometimes [*pause, thinking*] But I was taught to love everything on earth [*arms out to the skeletons*] I love you guys.

He hugs the tree.

THE PEDOPHILE: [*cheek against tree*] I don't recognize myself on a daily basis.

Then the muscles on his face slacken, and he rubs his face on the tree to see if he has feeling or not.

THE PEDOPHILE: I love everything.

The semen crowds his mouth. He pushes it back and hits himself in the throat, no look on his drooping face as he tries not to gag from the scrape of the hard sleeve. One hand on the tree to stand up.

[*Next Day.*]

More skeletons. The boy remains absent. Now, a black sphere hangs over the tree. And looking up at the tree, the pedophile stands, scratching his head and looking at his nails. He is very tired.

THE PEDOPHILE: They are still with me.

He blows lice off his nails.

[*Next Day.*]

The boy brings the rake down to the pedophile. In front of the tree, again wearing the garbagebag over his head, the pedophile stares at the skeletons.

THE PEDOPHILE: [*quietly, taking the rake*] There are so many.

He hits the thickly-wound skeletons but only loosens small chips. The chippings fall. He realizes he cannot get them down using only the rake anymore, so he climbs the tree and reaches out. He grabs a skeleton and starts shaking it. The rib cage of the skeleton is stuck around a branch, unmoving. And the pedophile shakes harder and harder until he falls from the branch, screaming at the skeleton from which he hangs by his hands. Eventually he pulls the skeleton free, and falls with it—to the boy's feet.

THE PEDOPHILE: [*on his back, looking up at the black sphere*] Do you have school tomorrow?

THE BOY: No, I have a three-day weekend [*holds two fingers up, then lifts the third with his other hand*] Three more days until I have school again.

THE PEDOPHILE: Good. That's good.

The pedophile stands slowly. He climbs the tree again, with the rake. He looks down at the boy, who is on one knee tying his boot.

THE PEDOPHILE: [*to himself*] Why doesn't he want to kiss me. Just split his small skull open with the metallic part of the rake. Just, there [*clears throat*] One hit would do it [*then louder*] Are you sure you don't want to kiss me? I'm a good kisser and my mouth is clean. I flossed the old food out of my mouth and swallowed it. My mouth is very clean why don't you want to kiss it? Oh. Are you sure you don't want to kiss my clean mouth? [*opens wider the mouthhole on the mask*]

THE BOY: [*looks up from boots*] I'm sure.

The pedophile rests in the skeleton web, with his hands behind his head.

THE PEDOPHILE: I hate to tell you this, but no one wants you here.

THE BOY: What? [*changes knee, ties other boot*] I don't understand what you're saying.

THE PEDOPHILE: I mean no one asked you to be here. Doesn't that bother you? Don't you feel mad about that? I am so embarrassed for you. You make me sick. Your parents are criminals but I am willing to call you my own. Do you want to kiss me and sleep with me in the plastic toilet on the side of the road?

The pedophile gets down from the tree and grabs the rake. He tightens his grip. The boy runs back up the hill. Negotiating the onset of tears, the pedophile returns to the work of cleaning the tree. Taking down the skeletons. There are so many now, and he looks at them like he isn't even sure he cares about doing it anymore, not at all sure.

THE PEDOPHILE: All I want to do is kiss someone.

[*Next Day.*]

The boy stands by the tree, looking around. From behind the tree, the pedophile speaks.

THE PEDOPHILE: [*wavering, phlegmatic*] I don't know what is happening. I don't.

THE BOY: What's wrong. It seems like something is wrong with you. Please tell me. I can help you.

THE PEDOPHILE: It's my face. My face feels numb. The numbness is traveling so deep. Like I would need to press my finger deep deep into my face to even feel it. I don't know what is happening to my face. I need help.

THE BOY: How do you need help? [*looks at black sphere and forgets what he is saying*] What if your face never feels like anything again? Would you still want it? Would you still want it at all?

THE PEDOPHILE: Maybe [*takes a few slow steps towards the boy*] Maybe, but I don't know. Maybe we should see if I still want this one. Maybe you should put your fingers on my face. Put your fingers on my face and press into it. Or you can let your tongue touch my tongue. We can put our mouths together. That would be nice too.

THE BOY: But what if I get the same way then? [*touches own face*] I like my face so much. It is so soft.

Semen drips from the pedophile's mouth. His face droops and the muscles die off. He rubs lice off his head. Some of the scabs lift with it, bleeding down his face. He stands, dripping semen from his mouth, brow muscles hanging over his eyes.

THE PEDOPHILE: I know it's soft. I want it [*wipes mouth with hand*] Give it to me you fucking faggot. I will make you stretched red and raw. Hurting. I will come in your body. And your muscles will droop too [*semen is all over his neck, the collar of his shirt wet with it, and his face turns black, drooping*] Stay here with me at the bottom of the hill. We can go into the woods and lie down on some wet leaves. I will clean you off with a leaf when I am done. When I am done things will be different. I will teach you about yourself. I am absolute hatred. Shake my hand and lie down with me—you are mine.

The boy makes a surprised look and jumps. He puts his hands on his head then on his ears then runs back up the hill. He trips towards the top but keeps running until he's gone. The pedophile watches, pulling at his own face with his hands.

THE PEDOPHILE: I have nothing [*letting hands go to his sides*] Being ugly is comfortable.

He stands there into the night. Days pass, represented by slow black flashes. There is snow during some of the flashes. Snow accumulates around the pedophile's feet. He stands completely still. Wind. Large white flies emerge from his mask and gravitate to the black sphere, become invisible.

THE PEDOPHILE: I love myself.

[*Next Day.*]

The branches are thick with skeletons, disregarded. And the rake is on the ground next to the tree, its prongs rusty and still somewhat capped with dust left from struck bones. The pedophile is not there.

[*Days Later.*]

The boy runs down the hill and stands by the tree. The pedophile is still gone. The boy looks around, quiet. He sits against the trunk, poking the snow and kicking it into piles. He gets up and unzips his pants, holds his shirt up with both hands. Then he pisses on the tree. The pedophile crawls out from the skeletons and then down the tree. No mask now. He sniffs the piss on the tree and drinks some that has pooled in a smashed can.

THE PEDOPHILE: [*stretching, eyes closed*] I smelled that you were here. You are the best. You are unbearable. I love you. The only reason I am glad to be alive is that you are alive too, at the same time [*leans face into tree*] You will appreciate your life when you understand that the people alive at the same time are yours by chance. Do you know that? I love you so much. When your piss is in my body I want to rip you in half [*he puts the garbagebag mask on and holds up his hands*] I am glad you are back. When I am alone I think that my soul is gone. I'm worried that I never had a soul. That is a huge worry of mine. No actually I'm worried that I'm stupid enough to have had any thoughts like that. [*smiles*] But not when I see your pretty face.

The boy kneels and spreads the snow out, humming to himself.

THE PEDOPHILE: Your face is beautiful and I am going to build a box around it so if I want to look in once in a while I can, but no one else can. I guess I have to lock the box around your head so no one else can look [*puts both hands palms towards the back of the boy's head*] If I rust the lock it will be more difficult to open [*puts palms towards sky*] And for me that is good. I hope I am not scaring you at all. I just want to keep your head in a box so it can be only mine. [*more flies burst and leave the eyeholes of his mask, disappear into the black sphere*]

THE BOY: [*turns around, still sitting*] Don't forget where you put the key.

THE PEDOPHILE: [*ignoring*] I want you to be in a little safe. Everyone has a little safe and they keep things in it. The things that you keep in your safe are different when other people look at them. But when only you look at them, they are perfect [*motherly, close*] What do you keep in it? Huh?

THE BOY: [*looking away*] I'm not telling. I can't tell you.

THE PEDOPHILE: Why not? Are you upset? Don't you like me? Don't you trust me at all? What if I shave my fingers long and thin and just reach through the keyhole? What would I feel? Would I feel something nice? Is your blood in there? Is your cute little head in there? I will make my arms and fingers thin enough to reach in. When you are thinner than the keyhole you don't need the key.

THE BOY: [*throwing snow into the air, watching it fall*] Don't touch me.

THE PEDOPHILE: When the flies first started being born from my head I was scared but now I feel good about it. I like that I'm their mommy. Hello. I am glad you found me. I was feeling unneeded. I was feeling far away from you. Don't you like being my friend? Why don't you visit me more? If you want to see me anymore, you will answer me. If you don't [*palms towards boy's face*] I will put my hand over your mouth until you hate me. Please answer me.

THE BOY: I don't like the way you smell [*backs away, face showing disgust*] Your mouth is too warm. It's hot on my face. I don't like how you smell. I hate it.

THE PEDOPHILE: [*walks towards the boy*] No my mouth is clean. And you can have it. Come here and have it. Come here.

THE BOY: You didn't say the magic word [*sneezes*] Say please. Please Louise.

The pedophile reaches out to touch the boy's face. Overeager though. His fingers hit the boy in the eye. The boy closes his eye tight, and squirms backwards over the leaves. He backs against the tree. He scrapes his neck on a broken branch. Bleeds.

THE BOY: You are not my friend anymore. [*one eye clenched, trying to smear the blood off his neck also*] Not anymore.

THE PEDOPHILE: [*face blackens*] I missed you. I didn't even know who I was. I missed you the whole time and didn't stop missing you for even two seconds. No one will bury you but me. If I want no one to find you, then no one will find you. I don't want you to call me your friend [*stops, staring at the boy*] I missed you so much. I thought about you all the time. I learned about my own face by staring at your pretty eyes. And I thought there was an eclipse. I prayed to God to help me find you. And God did. I found you. Do you want to [*pauses*] or wait—did you miss me?

The pedophile walks to the boy. He puts his fingers over the wound and wipes the blood into the snow. The boy groans and the pedophile stands, blocking the sunlight from the boy's head.

THE PEDOPHILE: This will help [*pointing and touching the wound*] Let me help you. The eclipse means everything is fine.

THE BOY: It stings when your finger touches me [*breathing deep*] That hurts. That hurts like a bug is biting me. Stop biting me you bug.

THE PEDOPHILE: No, I am making you feel better. Don't move.

THE BOY: [*coughs*] Is that why you missed me? Did you want to touch my neck?

THE PEDOPHILE: I wanted to touch your neck and put pretty cosmetics on your face. I wanted to make you presents and break your neck. Fucking crush your entire face and head into deflation. If I bathed my hands and face in the piss from your squirming and broken-necked body, I would never be sad again. Do you know that?

The pedophile kneels and puts his arm around the boy.

THE BOY: [*resting his head on the pedophile's belly*] When you are old and dead I will not visit you. I will put the rake away and never get it out again.

The pedophile runs his fingernails over where the blood is cooling and hardening. He scrapes some off and blows it to the ground.

THE BOY: Be careful [*seems to rest deeper, head on the pedophile's stomach*] Your nails are hurting me. You bug.

The boy lifts his arm up to the pedophile's face and touches it. The pedophile scrapes lice off his head and blows it onto the boy's face.

THE PEDOPHILE: Make a wish [*puts hand over boy's face*] I have nails because I am a growing boy. When the nails get bigger I know that I am getting bigger too. And that I am safe. Do you feel safe with me? I am the eclipse.

THE BOY: [*through the hand over his face*] Not feeling anything.

The pedophile continues to scrape off lice and comb it into the boy's hair with his fingers. They both fall asleep on the ground. They are not in love.

[*Next Day. Snowing.*]

In the tree there is a skeleton that still has a patch of hair and skin on its skull. The pedophile stares at it, holding the boy's hand.

THE PEDOPHILE: That's for you [*pointing up with the rake*] Look what I found for you. Do you want me to get it down? I will do that for you.

The boy nods. The pedophile retrieves the patch of hair, knocking it off with the rake-prongs. He secures the hair around the boy's throat with an old rubberband.

THE PEDOPHILE: I don't want anyone to touch your throat when I'm not there to see it or stop it.

The boy puts his fingers up to the rubberband and tries to loosen it. Then he runs away screaming. Gone from the clearing. The pedophile touches his face, standing underneath the tree. He eats segments off an icicle hanging from a skeleton. Then spits the segments at the trunk of the tree until he can't reach the icicle with his mouth anymore.

[*Next Day.*]

Into the clearing trips the boy. The pedophile is hiding behind the tree. He is not wearing the garbagebag over his head. And he has thick yolky scabs in the shaven parts of his head. His eyes are irritated from crying. The pedophile covers his face and the scabs. He hides behind the tree.

THE PEDOPHILE: Don't come by me, please.

The boy stands still. He breathes and watches the breaths. Holding the rake.

THE PEDOPHILE: Please don't come, I am very ugly to look at. I sometimes had this thought but now I am convinced I'm the ugliest person or thing that has ever been around. Oh God [*voice wavers, phlegmatic*] There are so many people and things in the world it seems hard to be the ugliest of them all. But, that is what I am. And there is no way to make something else uglier than me without retaining my ugliness through plotting something like that [*wavering again*] Oh God.

The boy eats some snow. The pedophile cries in little bursts, sniffing a lot. Behind the tree still.

THE PEDOPHILE: Don't come anymore. Just don't [*through the phlegm*] Do you hate me? Don't you hate me at all? [*speaking quickly*] I'm hideous. I'm in pain. I don't need the rake. Put the rake away. The tree is fine with them up there. They're fine up there. They are still with me. Go away [*looks at his hands, covered in yolk from the scabs, wipes hands on pants*] Sorry for being so mean to you. I'm, just upset about something. Please don't be mad [*shrieking*] Get away from me you fucking bitch [*calm*] This happens every year and every year I think it will be done.

The pedophile grinds his jaw, breathing heavily and poking his eyes. He shrieks pathetically. He knows that the worst person to be is him.

THE BOY: I am embarrassed. I don't know how to make you feel better. You're being very strange. I'm embarrassed. Why are you acting like this? Don't you want to be friends with me? [*walks over to the pedophile, touches the pedophile's leg*] Hey. You need to get better. We have to keep the tree clean [*walks to get rake*] I'll clean off the rake for you.

The pedophile kneels. He puts his face towards the snow, and the old wet leaves.

THE PEDOPHILE: The leaves feel good against my skull [*exasperated*] Why does anything ever happen [*pushing skull against ground*] Only I know what I see and think. They are still with me [*calmer*] Yeah the leaves feel good.

The boy stands over him, holding the rake in one hand. He unzips his pants and takes out his penis with the other hand. He pisses onto the pedophile, over the scabs and down his back. The boy looks at the tree and it seems like all the skeleton eyes are watching him, some sockets muddy and some looking straight through a broken skull to the sky behind. He shudders and continues pissing. The pedophile lifts his head and stares at the sky—the black sphere—and he folds his hands in prayer. There is piss across his face.

THE PEDOPHILE: Today they will try again. They will try to kill me. But it won't happen today. Today they will try to kill me. I will stop it today. Mother Mary, may those who try to kill me find me too dead to be touched and let them die instead and be carried away by your hands and may your hands be lined with sharp sticks and may you have no home for the people that die. Amen.

The boy shakes his penis off and tucks it back in.

THE BOY: Amen.

The pedophile grabs the boy's leg.

THE PEDOPHILE: Nothing will ever make me laugh again. If I ever laugh again it will be accidental. But I will have fun while I am here [*peels scab off head in long tear*] I will have enormous amounts of fun. And it will be hard to die because I will have loved everything so much [*laughs*] It's really terrible how fun everything is [*grabs other leg. firm voice*] You are the love of my life, and while you are sleeping I will sew our sleeves to the backs of each other's shirts, so we will be hugging all the time, or at least close enough to see each other's faces. You are a box and all boxes get opened up. The time is now to make you blind and break your neck [*face muscles droop, laughs*] The time is now to break the skull of one of the skeletons and slit your throat open, onto my bare feet.

He holds onto the boy's legs. The boy puts his hand over the pedophile's skull, as though blessing him.

THE BOY: Don't touch me.

THE PEDOPHILE: [*ignores*] I want you to have a present. I want to show you something and I want you to love it. Do you promise that you will love it? Huh do you promise? Come on [*releases the boy's legs, stands*] Come with me.

THE BOY: [*trying to back away*] There will be a day when no one smiles at all. I bet. There will be a day when no one smiles about anything. I bet.

The pedophile puts on his garbagebag mask then holds out his hand.

THE PEDOPHILE: Here. We have to go somewhere. For me to show you something. Your present. You'll like it. Come on. Come with me [*taking his hand*] I have no control over myself. I have no hope. I get even hornier when I know I don't care. I can't feel anything anymore but I want to try. Come with me real quick, just real quick. For me to show you something that you'll like. Come on. I have a present.

THE BOY: I don't want to touch your hand. I will follow you though. But you have to walk three steps ahead of me. Then I follow you.

They walk. Eventually they encounter a dog, tied to a stake at the bottom of a sloping backyard. The dog eyes them both.

THE BOY: [*looking at dog, addressing the pedophile*] I have hope in myself. And you have none. When I have the greatest hope in myself, you have none. I think that's why you're sad.

THE PEDOPHILE: Huh? [*looking at the dog*] Maybe. But I'll be here as long as you. Our time will be equal.

THE BOY: [*steps towards the dog then stops when it tenses*] But you look way more dead. And the flies are already eating you. I'll be here longer than you I bet. I'll be here until the day no one smiles.

THE PEDOPHILE: [*still staring at the dog*] Look at how pathetic this dog is. To me, this is you.

The boy watches his feet, pressing snow down with the toe of his boot. Avoiding the dog.

THE BOY: What do you have for me? You said you had something. What is it? [*pause*] Give it to me.

The pedophile takes the boy's hand and puts it top-down in the snow. The pedophile kneels on the boy's hand.

THE PEDOPHILE: I'm going to teach you a cool trick.

THE BOY: [*trying to pull out*] I don't like touching your hand. But thank you [*still trying to pull out*] Thank you but don't touch me.

The pedophile holds the boy's hand in the snow and kneels on it until the skin is numbed raw. Then he drags the boy to the dog and pokes the dog's mouth with the numb hand. The dog bites it. Eats the hand in stringy pulls. And the boy watches, feeling nothing.

THE BOY: [*staring at dog*] Thank you for teaching me this trick. I love it. Thank you. It's cool.

The pedophile continues to watch the dog eat the boy's hand.

THE PEDOPHILE: [*tenses*] You are polite for saying thank you. You are so polite [*seems agitated*] No problem.

The pedophile watches the dog swallow, increasingly agitated by the sight.

THE PEDOPHILE: God-damnit [*choking*] The dog troubles me. I can't stand it [*stands, hits head against thick tree nearby, four times solidly*] The dog is enjoying you [*almost falling*] It loves you. There is no sharing with a dog [*louder*] I have to have it back. I have to take it back. The dog is troubling me. I feel worse than I have ever felt, ever ever. No earth I stand on floats. Ever ever.

The muscles on his face drop. He takes out a plastic shopping bag from his pocket and wraps it around the dog's head and pulls the handles together. He tugs the handles tight a few times, the dog grunting with each tug. Then the pedophile lifts the bag in the air and throws it down, stepping on exposed legs. The pedophile breaks the dog's front legs, bending them with hard stomps.

THE BOY: [*staring at his own stripped-hand, nearly fainting*] I think I'm in love [*pause*] Thank you for teaching me that trick.

The pedophile picks up the crippled dog and throws it at the boy. With weight and what remain of its legs, the dog pins the boy down and attacks the boy's face and chest in confused aggression, biting through the plastic bag. The pedophile watches. He watches neck and face becoming nothing, as the boy yells into the clamping teeth of the dog, until death. And then the pedophile kicks the plasticbag-necklaced dog off the boy. He lifts the boy and carries him back to the tree, throwing the corpse up into the skeletons. Bright light comes from behind the black sphere. The pedophile sleeps, back of head against tree.

Sam Pink lives in Chicago, IL. He is the author of Person (Lazy Fascist Press), Frowns Need Friends Too (Afterbirth Books), and I Am Going to Clone Myself Then Kill the Clone and Eat It (Paperhero Press), You Hear Ambulance Sounds And Think They Are For You (Willows Wept Press), and Yum Yum I Can't Wait to Die (Jaguar Uprising).

His work has appeared in The Lifted Brow, Columbia Poetry Review, Exquisite Corpse, Slingshot, Pax Americana, Unsaid Magazine, Storyglossia, Lamination Colony, decomP, Everyday Genius, Robot Melon, Dogmatika, Pineapple War, No Colony, and many other publications.

Visit him online at impersonalelectroniccommunication.com.

CPSIA information can be obtained
at www.ICGtesting.com
Printed in the USA
FSOW01n1917251114
3578FS

9 781936 383351